Her Alpha Daddy Next Door

An Older Alpha Male, Younger BBW Romance

Nichole Rose

Contents

Dedication

To C. – Thanks for being the boss of me.

About the Book

He's not the boss of her...but he wants to be.

Carter

Luna Goodson is a mess.

She's too trusting, too innocent, and too hot to resist.

The first time I saw her, she insulted my parents.

The second time, she warned me that steroids cause shrinkage.

Lucky for her, I'm not into steroids. But I am into her.

She calls me Officer Grumpy. I want her to call me Daddy.

Now I just have to convince her to fall for me too.

Luna

When my older brothers boss me around, it's annoying.

When the hot detective downstairs does it, my entire body lights up like a Christmas tree.

Carter Grayson is big, grumpy, and rude...but when he calls me princess, I want to be so good for him.

He says he wants me to be his. I just hope he means forever-ever.

Because once he claims me, I don't want him to let me go.

Warning

When this older alpha male meets his younger BBW, all bets are off in this sweet, steamy romance from Nichole Rose. If instalove, crazy dogs, and over-the-top shenanigans aren't your thing, look away! All Nichole Rose books come complete with a sticky sweet and guaranteed HEA.

Chapter One

Carter

"The complex is quiet," Darren Danvers says, scratching his messy beard as he follows me from room to room in the downstairs apartment we're looking at. "We don't have many problems around here."

"Yet you want a cop on site," I murmur, prowling through the spacious two bedroom they're offering me for free in exchange for parking my cruiser out front and patrolling the property periodically. It's a good gig. The complex is full of young professionals and retirees. It's also located in a better part of the city, less than a mile from the precinct office where I'm stationed.

"You know how people are," Danvers says with a grin that suggests we're in on some big secret. We aren't. I don't particularly like Danvers. It's eight in the morning, but I'm almost positive he's drunk. His eyes are blood-shot. He squints at me like he's having trouble focusing. He's middle-aged and squirrely. But he isn't Layla Wallace...and that's about as big an endorsement as I can think of at the moment.

Layla may have been hot, but she was not mentally stable. She also had a key to my last apartment, thanks to her position as the property manager. A man can only come home from work so many times to an uninvited psycho in his bed before shit has to change. After I kicked her out yesterday, I decided it was time to get the hell out.

She did not take it well when I told her the sight of her made my dick shrivel. The truth hurts, I guess. But psycho doesn't do it for me. Hell, not much seems to do it for me these days. There are badge bunnies all over this city, and I'm not a bad looking guy. My job requires that I keep in shape, so I lift weights and run most days. At six-four and two-hundred and thirty pounds, I've always been on the big side...and women love guys my size. But my dick doesn't seem satisfied with any of them anymore. It's been months since I took anyone to my bed.

"So what do you think?" Danvers asks when I make a circuit through the master bedroom.

The apartment isn't bad at all. The master suite is killer. The walls are a soft white, and the carpet is plush and looks new. The windows are all north-facing, which means I won't be blinded by light during the day when I'm trying to sleep. The bathroom is massive, with a whirlpool tub and a separate shower.

"Tell me about the neighbors."

"There's a banker or something to your right and a reporter above him. They're rarely ever home. The girl directly above you is a real tight little piece." Danvers licks his lips, turning those blood-shot eyes on me. "She's young, with a massive rack and an ass for days."

I arch a brow, shoving my hands into my pockets to hide the way they clench. Why is it not surprising that this man is lusting after a girl probably decades younger than he is? Oh, right. Because he looks exactly like every other middle-aged pervert I've ever had the displeasure of meeting. And I've met a lot of them thanks to the fourteen years I've spent on the force. Even before I moved to Robbery and Homicide three years ago, I lacked faith in people. Nothing I've seen since has changed my mind any.

"She moved in a few days ago. She's something else." Danvers huffs out a breath, chuckling. "Has the worst damn luck of anyone I've ever met. Always needing something fixed or looked at."

Right. Or maybe he just intentionally doesn't fix shit properly so he can wheedle his way into her apartment more often. More than likely, she's an average girl. But to a man like him, with beady eyes, a bushy beard, and a beer gut, any hole's a goal.

"She's a real sweet thing. Won't give you any problems." His gaze flicks up and down me in rapid assessment. "You might be more her type than I am," he says with another buddy-grin. "I imagine you do fine with the ladies."

I snort instead of answering. Anyone is probably more this girl's type than Darren Danvers, but I don't tell him that. I make a mental note to keep an eye on the girl, make sure he isn't harassing her or making her uncomfortable. If she's as young as he says, the last thing she needs is some dirty old man invading her personal space at every available opportunity.

I don't particularly want to have to look after a teenager, but it is what it is. Dirty Danvers and the girl upstairs are a sight better than Psycho Layla.

A memory of her screeching at me as I tossed her clothes at her plays through my mind, making my head throb. Jesus. I didn't even know the human voice registered at that octave. She sounded like a dying cat.

"I'll take it," I decide, shuddering at the memory.

Loud hip-hop blares through the apartment, jolting me awake. I sit upright in my bed, cursing beneath my breath as Biggie's voice reverberates off the walls. Grabbing my smartwatch from the nightstand, I see that it's barely noon.

I've been in bed for all of three hours after getting home late, thanks to an early morning robbery. And I've gotta be back in at six for another twelve-hour shift before I get a day off. I spent all of yesterday moving my shit in before work. It's still in boxes, and I'm fucking exhausted.

I glare up at the ceiling, silently willing the girl upstairs to turn the music down. As if the Universe is flipping me the proverbial bird, the music gets louder instead.

"Son of a bitch," I curse, throwing the covers back and climbing from the bed. I grab a pair of sweats off the floor and yank them on, not even bothering with underwear. I shove my feet into a pair of tennis shoes before stomping through the apartment and out the front door.

I don't even close it behind me. It's bright as hell outside, which pisses me off even more. Sunshine and I don't mix. I've worked nights most of my life. I'm used to darkness and quiet. Not Biggie and sunshine.

The entire metal stairway shakes as I climb it two at a time. Oddly, the music isn't that loud out here. The walls between apartments must be paper thin. Which is just fucking great for me. I'll be able to hear every damn sound my neighbors make.

When I reach the landing and get a sight of the girl's door, my scowl deepens. Potted plants, with fairies and dragons scattered throughout the greenery, line the balcony outside her red door. A little hobbit house hangs above, with a hole for birds. Even her doormat is *Lord of the Rings* inspired. The damn thing says, "Speak, friend, and enter." in a fancy script.

"You gotta be kidding me," I groan when I see the door knocker is a dragon. There's no way this chick is as hot as Danvers said she was. She's a legitimate nerd. If I weren't so tired, I'd appreciate that fact. I like a woman with a mind.

I forego using the knocker and pound on the door.

"Just a minute!" she yells from inside, her voice soft and sweet. A couple of seconds later, the music, thankfully, shuts off.

I wait impatiently for her to open the door. She does less than ten seconds later...not nearly long enough for her to have checked her peephole. Hell, she doesn't even ask who I am. She just throws the door wide open, almost tumbling out in the process.

She catches herself using the doorjamb. I rake my gaze down her body.

Jesus Christ.

Danvers wasn't lying. She's fucking hot.

Glossy black hair hangs in curls down her back, framing her heart-shaped face. Thick lashes frame her wide blue eyes. She's dressed in a t-shirt and the smallest pair of shorts I've ever seen...neither of which does anything to hide her incredible body. She's petite and curvy with a soft stomach and thick thighs. She barely reaches my chest.

"Oh," she whispers, blinking those big blue eyes at me. Her tongue peeks out, sweeping along her bottom lip as she looks me over. Her cheeks flush a soft pink.

"Fuck me." I rake a hand through my hair, staring at her as my dick turns to steel. There's no hiding the damn thing. He just pops up, pointing right at her like he wants to get better acquainted. I think the rest of me does too. She's too goddamn sexy, and she's into nerdy shit.

I haven't had nearly enough sleep to comprehend how absolutely fucked I am.

"You're huge," she blurts out.

A surprised bark of laughter rumbles from my lips.

Her eyes go comically wide. "Um, I mean, you're very big. Not your..." She waves in the direction of my dick. "Though it's not exactly small either. I mean, wow! You must have won all the penis measuring contests, huh? Um. I didn't mean your penis is huge, though. I mean you. Tall. Big. I could climb you like a tree. You probably lift weights and stuff." Her cheeks flush brighter, the pink color crawling down to her neck and then disappearing beneath the collar of her shirt...which doesn't help my dick situation.

I bet she's pink everywhere. I want to strip her down and see if I'm right. I'd make it worth her time. Have her leaving claw marks up and down my back.

"I tried to lift weights once, but I wasn't very good at it," she says. "Those things are a lot heavier than they look. But you look like you could probably lift a lot of them. You're big all over. Even your...um...Is it always like that? I mean, Jesus. How do you walk with it like that?"

I laugh loudly as she rambles, digging herself deeper. Jesus Christ, she's a mess.

Eventually, she clamps her lips shut and drops her head toward her chest, groaning. "I'm going to shut up now." She shakes her head and takes a deep breath, seemingly marshaling her thoughts. Once she's more or less composed, she tips her head back to look up at me. "Can I help you?"

God, I hope so. Because my dick is going to break in half if he gets any harder for her. Her talking him up like he's a world champion did not help the situation. He's all for picking her up, wrapping her legs around my waist, and plowing into her until she's screaming daddy at the top of her lungs for me.

No. No fucking way.

She's maybe nineteen or twenty. Way too young for me.

"The music," I mutter, sobering at the reminder. "It's too goddamn loud."

"What music?" She blinks up at me again like she's genuinely confused.

"Biggie."

"You know Biggie?"

I cock a brow at her. "He's more my generation than yours."

"How old are you?" Christ, she's cute, eyeing me like she finds my statement suspicious or something.

"Thirty-five. How old are you?"

"Twenty-one." She frowns up at me. "His first album released in 1994. You were ten. Your parents let you listen to Biggie when you were ten? That's terribly unhealthy. He talked about sex an awful lot on that album."

"Christ," I mutter, shaking my head. This chick is something else. "Just turn it down. I'm trying to sleep below you."

"In the middle of the day?"

"I work nights."

"Are you a gigolo?"

I chuckle again. "No. Detective."

"Oh. Sorry, officer." She smirks when she says it, like she's fucking with me. "I didn't know anyone had moved in. I'll turn it down."

"Thanks." I start to leave and then pause, looking her over again. "You should check your peephole before you answer the door."

"It's the middle of the day."

"Criminals don't care what time it is."

"They probably aren't very good criminals then," she mumbles, making me shake my head again. She's far too damn innocent to be out here on her own.

"Just check the peephole."

"Fine." She scowls at me, which is just fucking cute.

Jesus.

"Are you going to be a problem?"

She slams her hands down on her hips and tips her head back, hitting me with an offended glare that makes my dick twitch again. "I've never been a problem in my entire life. Are *you* going to be a problem?"

Fuck. I think I'm in love.

"Yeah," I mutter with a soft chuckle as I walk away. "You're definitely going to be a problem."

And I am so looking forward to it.

Chapter Two

Luna

"I still don't know about you living in Los Angeles by yourself, little bird," my mom says into the phone. "Maybe I should send your brothers down for a few days to make sure everything is okay for you."

"Mama, I'm fine," I mutter into the phone, rolling my eyes while I pet my Yorkie, Peter. I named him after Peter Jackson, who is kind of my idol. Peter is sprawled across my lap with his legs straight up in the air, soaking up the attention. He's shameless. He also thinks he's a big guard dog. He has a problem with people who aren't me.

"Your brothers would love to see you," she says.

"You mean they would love to drag me back home." I love my brothers like crazy, but they are seriously overprotective. They chased away every boy who was ever interested in me. I guess that's what happens when you're the youngest and the only girl with three older brothers. But yeesh! They're the reason I decided to move over three hours away from home after graduating from college a few weeks ago. I'll never find my own way with three older brothers breathing down my neck.

"They love you."

"I love them too, but I'm not ready to come home, Mama. I'm doing just fine on my own."

My mom makes a sound of dismay, like she doesn't believe me. Not that I blame her. I'm kind of a hot mess. I can take care of myself, but I have a mouth that runs way ahead of my brain, and I try to see the good in everyone. It gets me into trouble sometimes.

"My new neighbor is a cop," I say, knowing she'll love that. I leave out the part about him being really hot and really grumpy. But Lord, the man is gorgeous with his dark hair, wicked green eyes, and dimple. I *could* probably climb him like a tree. Although I probably shouldn't have said that to him.

"Oh, really?" my mom asks. "That's great, Luna!" She chatters on, but I tune her out, thinking about Officer Grumpy downstairs.

I almost fell over when I opened the door the other day and saw him standing there without a shirt on. His body is ripped. I wanted to lick him...and then he got hard, and I wanted to wrap my legs around his waist and do really dirty things to him.

The reminder makes my cheeks burn. I can't believe I said he was huge. I wasn't even talking about his penis the first time, but I might as well have been. It was pretty huge too. And really hard. I'm not sure if he was hard because of me or what, but I hope it was me. He definitely had my panties wet. Not that I'm going to tell him that. He was kind of rude.

Though I do feel bad for waking him up. I always play my music loud when I'm working. Everyone else in our building works during the day, so it's never bothered anyone before. I've tried to be quieter for the last couple of days, but it's a lot harder than I expected. I feel like a super spy sneaking around my apartment on my tiptoes so I don't wake up Officer Grumpy.

I should make him cookies. Then maybe he won't get mad next time I'm too loud. Which I probably will be. My entire family is loud and boisterous. I don't know how to be quiet. I tried to Google it, but I think Google thought I meant I wanted to be Zen or something because it kept giving me all these results about being quiet in my mind. Like that will ever happen.

"I'm going to make him cookies," I blurt out.

Mom stops chattering and is silent for a full minute.

"Did the call drop?" I ask, pulling the phone away from my face to check. Nope. We're still connected. I guess she's processing.

Peter rolls over and jumps from my lap, heading toward the kitchen in search of food. He barks twice. I climb to my feet and follow behind him. Like I expected, he's sitting in front of his bowl, waiting impatiently for me to fill it for him.

I shake my head at him and pull his food down, filling the bowl.

"You're making him cookies?" Mom finally asks.

"Yes? I mean, maybe?" I frown, wandering around my kitchen. "Should I not do that? I've never had neighbors before. Aren't you supposed to make your new neighbors cookies to say welcome to the neighborhood? Or the apartment complex, I guess." I huff out a breath, slapping a wayward strand of hair away from my face.

"Did you make your other neighbors cookies?"

"No?" I grimace, already knowing the jig is up. I divert her attention before she can start match-making. Officer Grumpy might be hot and make my lady bits happy, but he's grumpy. I can't do anything with grumpy. It's the complete opposite of everything I know. "My music may have woken him up," I admit. "He was grumpy about it. And then I may have insulted his parents for how he was raised?"

"Oh, Luna." My mom laughs quietly. "What am I going to do with you?"

"Love me?"

"Always, little bird. Always. Make him cookies and tell him you're sorry. If he's worth your time, he'll forgive you. If he's not, then that's his loss."

"Okay," I agree because she's right. She usually is. "Love you."

"Love you too, sweetpea. I'll call to check on you later."

"Tell dad and the boys I said hi. And that they aren't allowed to come down here to check on me without permission!" I roll my sleeves up and start pulling stuff out of the cabinets to make cookies. Luckily, I've been able to get everything unpacked and put away since I moved in last week. The apartment is really starting to look and feel like home to me.

I miss my crazy family, but I like having my own space and getting to make my own rules. The apartment is pretty spacious, which is great since I don't go out much. I prefer to stay indoors and laze around when I'm not working on something. I'm an illustrator, and I do graphic design work, too, so I spend most of my time at my desk or in front of my laptop.

"I'll keep them out of your hair," Mom promises. "Good luck!"

I hang up and set the phone on the island before turning to look at Peter. "You want to help me make cookies?" I ask him.

He stops eating long enough to turn his head in my direction and give me a look of disdain.

"Fine then," I mutter to him. "You're not getting any peanut butter."

He ignores me, which isn't surprising. I'm not a very good liar. Of course he's getting peanut butter. He's definitely the boss of me. He may be small, but he's a bully. And I'm a pushover. I can't help it. I like to make people—and Peter—happy.

"So what kind of cookies does Officer Grumpy like?" I ask.

Peter ignores me again, of course.

Two hours later, I've made a batch of each of the staples—chocolate chip, peanut butter, and snickerdoodle. I've also changed into a pair of cute shorts with lace on the bottom and a matching top. I consider putting on makeup, but decide to keep it low-key and only swipe on a little mascara and some lip gloss.

I'm kind of hoping Officer Grumpy isn't home, and I can just drop the cookies at the door and make my escape without having to talk to him again. That way, if he doesn't like the cookies, he doesn't have to pretend to enjoy them just to spare my feelings. His body is literal perfection, so he might not even eat cookies. Maybe I should have just made him a salad or something.

"Stop stalling," I tell myself.

Peter runs around in circles at my feet while I slip on some ballet flats. I hate to break his heart, but he's not going with me. He doesn't like new people, and I don't want Officer Grumpy to really hate me if Peter decides to try to bite him or pee on his leg...either of which is possible. Peter is kind of a savage.

"I'll take you out for a walk when I get back," I promise him before grabbing the plate of cookies out of the kitchen and heading for the door. I quickly turn around and go back to the kitchen to write Grumpy a note in case he isn't home.

Officer Grumpy (or should I call you Detective Grumpy?),

Sorry I woke you up. And insulted your parents for letting you listen to Biggie when you were a kid. I'm sure your parents are great and that you're a totally healthy adult with no serious hang-ups as a result of listening to Biggie too young.

I pause with my pen poised over the paper, trying to decide if I should add an apology for asking if he's a gigolo. Is that offensive even though I asked because he's definitely hot enough to have woman paying him to touch his giant penis? I'm not sure. I decide to leave it off and hope he's forgotten I asked.

Also, sorry in advance for any other noises you might hear. I'll try very hard to be quiet.

Don't eat these if you're allergic to any of the good stuff like wheat or nuts or milk or chocolate.

NOT a Problem,

Luna

So maybe I should leave off the *problem* part of the signature, but I'm not going to do it. He did insult me, after all. I'm not a problem, whatever that means. I'm the definition of not a problem. He's just grumpy and rude. And hot.

Christ on a cracker, I hope he's not married or in a relationship. This could get awkward if I knock on his door with cookies and some beautiful woman opens the door. There's no way I can compete with a supermodel, and he probably dates them. I mean, he's definitely gorgeous enough to pull that off with no problem.

I'm a solid size sixteen on a good day, with boobs I can't tame and a big butt. When I was younger, my body used to bother me, but I eventually learned to live with the fact that I'm short and curvy. It's just the way God made me. I get plenty of exercise and I'm healthy. Isn't that what really matters?

Before I can talk myself out of it, I hurry toward the door and dash outside with the note and cookies in hand. It's late afternoon, but the parking lot is still mostly empty. My stomach dips when I see Officer Grumpy's car parked in the spot designated for his apartment. I guess he is home and I'll have to face him.

I mean...I can't just set the cookies on the ground, ring his doorbell, and then run away. Can I?

I pause for a minute to consider the option and then discard it. It seems kind of cowardly, and I'm not a coward. Okay, maybe that's a lie. But I'm only nervous because I talked about his penis the first time I met him.

"Don't mention his penis," I coach myself as I walk down the steps, carefully balancing the plate so it doesn't crash to the ground. The banister railing is loose, so I walk slow to make sure I don't end up breaking my neck. Wouldn't that be an awful way to die? Trying to deliver cookies to the hot detective downstairs. He'd probably be really grumpy then.

His blinds are all drawn tight, and his front door is closed.

I stand outside it for a long moment, trying to work up the nerve to knock.

"Stop stalling and do it already."

"Do what?"

I scream as his deep, sexy voice sounds behind me. My arms go up, the plate of cookies flying into the air. I watch in stunned horror as gravity immediately takes hold of the plate and sends it plummeting toward the cement.

Surprisingly, the plate never hits the ground, and neither do any of the cookies. Officer Grumpy grabs the plate out of midair. The cellophane holds, keeping the cookies safely on the platter...probably because I wrapped half a box around the thing. It's not my fault. There is no taming cellophane. It's a design flaw, I swear.

"Holy shit," I whisper, blinking at Officer Grumpy. "You're like Batman. A really hot, really grumpy Batman."

Officer Grumpy throws his head back and laughs loudly.

I feel my cheeks heat with embarrassment. Why don't words ever stay in my head where they're supposed to stay? It's not really fair that they just come tumbling out without my permission.

"These for me, sweetness?" he asks, cocking a brow at me. Even in clothes, he's hot.

"Yes. Here." I shove the note at him, practically hitting him in the chest in the process.

He catches my wrist in his free hand, sending sparks shooting up and down my arm. I expect him to let me go once he keeps me from accidentally punching him, but instead, he just holds onto me. I tip my head way back to look up at him.

"Jesus," he mutters, staring at me like he can't figure out what to do with me. "You really are tiny, aren't you? Like a little fairy princess."

"Am not," I mumble, licking my lips. He smells like brandy and pine needles. The combination is oddly erotic. "I'm normal sized. You're just big."

His lips tip into a wicked smirk, revealing the dimple in his left cheek. "I think we established that last time, princess."

My cheeks flame with embarrassment at the reminder of our last meeting. "We're pretending that didn't happen, remember?"

"We are?" His grin widens.

"Yes, definitely." I bob my head up and down for emphasis. "Never happened."

"Well, princess, my dick is going to be sorely disappointed to hear that you never called him huge," Officer Grumpy says. "Especially since he seems to like you."

"He has good taste. I'm very likable."

"That so?"

I nod again, tugging on my arm to get it back. Does he even remember that he's holding it like I'm a hostage or something?

"Are you going to let me go?" I ask when he tightens his grip instead of releasing me.

"I haven't decided yet."

"Isn't it illegal to hold people hostage?"

"Is it?"

"You should know. You're the detective. By the way, am I supposed to call you Officer Grumpy or Detective Grumpy? I'm not sure which is appropriate."

"You think I'm grumpy?"

"You don't think you're grumpy?" I narrow my eyes on him, highly suspicious that he doesn't know he's grumpy and kind of rude. "You're also kind of rude."

Why does he keep smiling at me like that?

"That why you made me cookies?"

"No," I huff, rolling my eyes at him. "I made you cookies to say sorry for waking you up. And for insulting your parents. And also because being quiet is a lot of work, and I'm not very good at it, so these are preemptive strike cookies."

"You've been very quiet the last few days."

"I know!" I beam up at him, rather pleased with myself. And grateful that he noticed my effort because, good Lord! That was a lot of work. "See? I'm not a problem at all. You're just grumpy and rude. And you're still holding me hostage."

"Doesn't count," he mutters, narrowing his eyes on me.

"Why not?"

"Because you don't want me to let you go."

"I told you I did."

"You're a terrible liar, princess." He tugs me closer to his big body, reeling me in like I'm a catfish on a hook. "You're all flushed, and your heart is racing. I bet your panties are wet too. I think you like being my hostage."

Wow. He's pretty good at this detective stuff. Not that I'm telling him that.

"Do not," I lie. For good measure, I tug on my arm again. Not that it helps or anything. I think he could probably keep me here forever if he wanted to do it. "Hasn't anyone ever told you that steroids will make your um...penis shrink?"

He blinks at me, his mouth popping open. "You think I'm on steroids?"

"Either that or you're the Hulk." I wonder if his penis got bigger when he hulked out or if it's always been that size? I briefly consider asking him and then decide I probably shouldn't. It seems like an awfully personal question.

He stares at me for a full five count and then laughs again, only it sounds more like a laugh-groan than a real laugh. "Jesus Christ, you're going to ruin me, princess."

"Am not," I mutter, slightly offended, and a little bit turned on. I like when he calls me princess. It makes me feel like he thinks I'm something important. "You could probably eat all those cookies and still look like someone carved you. Which really isn't fair, by the way."

"What isn't fair?"

"You being all hot." Crap. I did not mean to say that.

He laughs again. "I'm pretty sure if I eat all these, I'll go into a diabetic coma."

"Oh no!" I gasp, dismayed. "You're diabetic?"

"No, I'm not diabetic." He rubs his fingers across my arm like he's trying to comfort me. The motion causes goosebumps to climb up my arm. "I fucking love cookies."

"Oh." I smile, relieved. "That's good then. I love them too. I don't eat them very often, though. They aren't good for me."

"If you even think about suggesting you're fat, I'm spanking your sexy ass," he growls.

Oh wow. I think I just had a mini-orgasm.

"Um..." I trail off, caught between the desire to say *yes, please* to the spanking and the urge to flee upstairs to the relative safety of my apartment. I've never been spanked before. Actually, I've never been *anything'd* before. I think I'd like it if he spanked me, though. Which probably isn't a good thing because I don't even know his name. "What's your name?"

"Carter Grayson."

"I'm Luna Goodson."

"You're kidding me," he mumbles and then immediately shakes his head. "Of course you aren't kidding. Fuck. You're definitely going to ruin me."

"Stop saying that!"

"It's true."

"It's rude."

He smirks at me again, showing off that dimple, but he doesn't say anything. We just stand there for a moment, staring at each other. His green eyes rove across my face like he's memorizing it. He still has a hold of my arm, which is kind of nice. Especially when he runs the rough pad of his finger across my skin.

I wonder if he'd spank me if I asked nicely?

"Peter!"

"What?"

"I have to go. Peter is waiting for me." I tug on my arm again. This time, he lets me go. His entire expression changes, his brows snapping together until he's glowering at me like I just broke the law or something. Which is crazy because I don't think needing to take my dog out before he pees on the carpet is a crime.

Carter seems to think so. He takes a step away from me and then another. "Thanks for the cookies," he mutters and then stalks toward his apartment.

I watch him for a minute, not sure what I did to make him mad this time. And then I shrug, deciding that grumpy is just his nature.

Why does that turn me on so much?

Chapter Three

Carter

"Luna," I moan, jacking my cock to images of her sprawled out beneath me, her sexy ass in the air while I eat her from behind. I bet she tastes even better than those fucking cookies. All sweet like sugar. She'll probably be soaked for me, too, crying out my name and babbling nonsense as I eat her alive. As soon as she's done coming all over my face, I'll plow into her, not stopping until she's screaming the walls down around us.

God, I already know she's going to be virgin tight and wild for it.

I picture her above me, her big tits jiggling in my face while she bounces on my cock, calling me daddy. Her blue eyes are wide, her full lips parted. Her skin is flushed pink all the way from her cheeks to her tight little cunt. She's begging me to come in her...to breed her.

"Fuck, Luna," I groan loudly as my balls draw up, and I come hard. I keep stroking to the image of her riding me until the last drop splashes against the shower floor and then washes down the drain. I tip my head back, panting for breath and cursing myself.

I've been getting off to filthy fantasies of her since she made my cock sit up and beg for attention the day I met her. Her bringing me those damn cookies two days ago didn't help. My dick is raw, but I'll think about her in passing, and it goes rock hard all over again. It's starting to piss me off.

She has a man.

"Fucking Peter," I growl, quickly scrubbing up and then turning the water off. I bet *Peter* doesn't even know what to do with a girl like Luna. He probably pumps into her twice and then comes before passing out, not even caring if she gets off or not.

I'd do her right. Treat her like the princess she is. I'd have her creaming on my cock day and night. The only time I'd stop fucking her would be to spoil her. If I was her daddy, she'd have whatever the hell she wanted. I damn sure wouldn't pass out before she got off. Repeatedly.

She's too good for Peter.

I've been stalking my window like a lunatic for the last two days, hoping to catch sight of the pencil dick who's with my girl, but I haven't seen him yet. I guess he shows up after I leave for work and hits the road after he gets what he wants from her. The thought alone pisses me off, but I suppose his hit it and quit it attitude is probably for the best. Going to jail for punching some kid is bound to have repercussions of the career-ending variety.

My job may be shit most of the time, but I do actually enjoy what I do.

I dry off quickly, tossing my towel toward the hamper. I don't bother getting dressed, instead heading straight toward my bed. Last night was another long one, with two robberies and a homicide back to back. Luckily, my number wasn't up in rotation, so any assistance I rendered was strictly of the teamwork variety. I'm still wiped, though.

It's hard not to be when I've been spending my downtime alternatively fucking my hand and trying to get a glimpse of the fuckwit dating my princess.

Before I make it halfway across the room, a sound from upstairs halts me in my tracks. She's been so quiet since the Biggie incident. I've barely heard a peep out of her. Which I'm honestly relieved about. Her note said she might get loud. If I had to hear her moaning Peter's name, I would have lost my damn mind.

"Peter, stop it," Luna says, her sweet voice loud. "I'm not kidding. Get off of me!"

Oh, hell no.

"I don't feel good, and you stink!" she cries, clearly frustrated with her asshole boyfriend. "Ugh! You're impossible. Would you go away and leave me alone?"

My girl doesn't feel good, and Pencil Dick Peter is hounding her? I'm going to fucking murder him and then hide his body where no one will ever think to look for him. I reverse course toward the closet and grab a pair of sweats, yanking them on as quickly as possible.

"Oh my God. Please go away," she whimpers like she's hurting.

The pained sound cracks my heart right in half.

"I'm coming for you, princess," I mutter, grabbing my badge and gun off the dresser. I don't even bother with shoes this time. Instead, I rush through the apartment, flinging the door open so hard it hits the wall and bounces back toward me. I catch it with my elbow, cursing when pain instantly shoots up my arm.

"Son of a whore!" I growl, slamming the door closed and then jogging toward the steps. I try to avoid stepping on the sun-fried worms littering the cement, but they're all over the damn place. The stairway shakes and rattles as I pound up the steps, not stopping until I'm in front of Luna's door.

My heart races as adrenaline and worry for her course through my veins. I swear to God if Peter hurt her, I really will kill him. Going to prison will be worth it if it means keeping that bastard from assaulting my girl.

"Police! Open up!" I yell, pounding hard enough to rattle the door in its frame.

A little dog yips from inside the apartment. I didn't even know she had a dog. Poor little princess really has been going out of her way to keep from waking me up. Once she's safe, I'm going to tell her she can make all the damn noise she wants.

"Open the door before I kick it in!" Shit. I should have put my shoes on. The door isn't particularly heavy, but kicking it in without shoes is going to hurt like a motherfucker.

"Don't you dare!" Luna shouts from inside. If I wasn't so worried about her, I'd smile at how offended she seems by the prospect of me kicking down her door.

"Luna, open the damn door!"

"Hold your horses, Grumpy! Jeez!" The lock clicks, and then she flings the door open. I take half a second to appreciate the sight of her in a tiny tank top and the world's smallest pair of shorts. Her tits press obscenely against the thin fabric of the top, and her shorts are wedged between her plump pussy lips in the greatest camel-toe of all time. Her hair is all mussed up, and her face is pale and drawn, but she doesn't look hurt. Thank God.

"Are you hurt, sweetness?"

"What?"

"Where the fuck is he?" I growl, stomping into her apartment.

"Who?" she asks.

"Peter. I'm going to kill him."

"Don't you threaten my Peter!" she yelps from behind me.

I whirl around to face her, scowling. "Your Peter just tried to assault you, Luna. I heard everything. Now tell him to get his sorry ass out here before I decide to kill him instead of just hauling him in."

She blinks up at me. Her mouth opens and closes a few times. And then her expression softens, and she bites her lip like she's trying not to laugh. "You can't take him to jail, Carter."

"The hell I can't," I growl.

She grimaces and presses a hand to her temple.

A little of my anger dissipates, unable to stand when she's in pain. As soon as I deal with Peter, I'll get her back into bed. My poor princess obviously has a migraine.

"Peter, no!" she cries, her eyes going wide.

I spin around just in time to see a streak come darting out of the bedroom. Half a second later, a set of teeth close around the leg of my pants. Her dog snarls like a savage beast as he shakes his head back and forth, latched onto my sweats the entire time.

"Peter! Stop it right this second!" Luna stumbles toward me.

"Peter?"

Jesus Christ. Is she telling me that Peter is a fucking dog? Actually, the animal currently trying to bite me doesn't even classify as a dog. He's smaller than one of my shoes. He's a savage little thing, though.

I reach down and scoop him up in one hand. He snarls and growls at me and then seems to realize I'm a lot bigger and meaner than him because he whimpers and then goes limp, flopping over in my hand like I killed him or something.

"Peter! You wicked little bully," Luna scolds, glaring at him with her hands on her hips and her tits heaving against that thin tank top. "I told you that you can't just go around biting people. It's not nice!"

He cracks one eye open and looks at me, and then rolls it in her direction before slamming it closed again. His tongue lolls out of his mouth like he's dead. I swear to God he's grinning, though. He really is a wicked little shit.

Luna takes him from me and sets him on the floor. "Go use the bathroom and come right back!" she demands, huffing at him. She's fucking hot when she's all riled up.

Peter races out the door without a backward glance.

"I'm so sorry," Luna whispers, putting her head in her hands. "Please don't take him to puppy jail. I swear he's harmless. He's just really protective, and he has little man syndrome because everything on the planet is bigger than he is. It makes him cranky."

"Just so we're clear...Peter is the dog?"

"Yes."

"And you don't have a man in here?"

"No. Well, you're here."

Thank fucking God for that.

I drop my badge and gun on her table.

"Hey! What are you doing?" she yelps when I swing her up into my arms. She doesn't try to fight me, though. Instead, she wraps her arms around me and clings. Her head lolls against my shoulder, making it clear she's in more pain than she's letting on.

I grit my teeth at the feel of her curves against my body. She's soft and lush everywhere. My dick immediately turns to steel, jerking in my sweats like he's trying to beat his way free to get at her. He won't be doing that, though. Not right now anyway.

"Where's your room, princess?"

"Why? I'm not sleeping with you."

The outright suspicion in her voice makes me smile.

"Not yet, you aren't," I mumble, grinning down at her as I stride through her apartment. "But you will most definitely be sleeping with me soon, Luna."

She huffs but doesn't disagree. She also doesn't tell me where her room is, but I find it easily enough. Her apartment is identical to mine, though hers is a lot nicer than mine. All of her shit looks brand new and expensive. Most of mine came from IKEA, mostly because I couldn't be bothered to find anything else. Why bother when it's always been just me?

That'll be changing soon.

"Jesus Christ," I mumble when I catch sight of her room. Dragons and fairies and every other fantasy creature ever thought up adorn her walls in vivid illustrations. Some are so detailed they look real. Her sleigh bed is massive, the purple sheets and blankets all twisted up. Everything else in the room is a soft white color, which makes the artwork even more eye-catching.

I carry her to the bed and lay her in it. It takes all my willpower not to crawl in beside her, but I can't do that yet. I need to deal with her crazy little dog and get her taken care of first. She rolls onto her side, snuggling into her pillow.

"Have you taken anything for your migraine, princess?" I ask, digging my hand into her thick mass of hair to massage her scalp.

"Not yet," she mumbles and then gives me a breathy little moan that makes my dick jerk in my sweats again. Jesus. I can't wait to hear her make that sound when I'm balls deep inside her.

"Where's your medicine?"

"I can get it."

"Luna, tell me where it's at," I order, keeping my voice soft. She's already had too much excitement and noise this morning.

"Top drawer on the left."

I gently untangle my hand from her hair and go get her medicine. It takes everything I have not to prowl through her panties like a pervert, but I don't do it. I'm nothing like Dirty Danvers. I mean, I may be a little kinky and want her to call me daddy, but I'm not creepy or a pervert. Besides, I plan on planting my kid in her and marrying her as soon as humanly possible.

Once I have her pills, I grab a glass of water and a cool washcloth from the bathroom and take them to her, making sure she takes her medicine and swallows half the water before I lay her back down and place the cool cloth over her eyes.

She doesn't say anything the entire time.

"Poor little princess." I lean forward and press my lips to her cheek before pulling her sheet up over her. Before I even stand up, she's asleep, soft little breaths puffing from her lips. I watch her for a moment, my heart pulsing with what I'm pretty certain is love, and then I go to retrieve her dog.

Peter is in the yard below, chasing a lizard. I grab my gun and badge and carry them back down to my apartment. He follows me in, racing all over the place and smelling everything. I shake my head at him, grab my keys, and then a pair of shoes before I scoop him up.

He growls at me once and then settles down, allowing me to carry him back to Luna's apartment. As soon as I put him down, he races to the kitchen and then yips like he expects me to follow him.

I find him sitting in front of an empty dish, waiting expectantly.

"You're a spoiled little shit, aren't you?" I mutter, poking through the cabinets until I find his food. Once I've overfilled the dish, I drop my keys on the counter and head toward Luna's room. I strip down before climbing in beside her.

"Carter," she sighs in her sleep and then wraps her sexy little body around me.

Yep. I'm definitely getting her pregnant and marrying her.

I pass out wearing nothing but a giant smile.

Chapter Four

Luna

I wake up disoriented, with a very large, very hot body wrapped around mine. For a moment, I think the thing poking me in the back is Peter...and then Carter mumbles something in his sleep, alerting me to the fact that it's definitely not my bully of a dog. Carter is in bed with me.

Holy crap. Carter is in bed with me.

My entire body freezes before I quickly glance down. I'm still fully clothed, though one of his big hands cups my left breast possessively.

Part of me wants to stay right where I'm at, but the rest of me really needs to pee. It also wonders why he's in my bed instead of downstairs in his own apartment. Not that I'm complaining very much. He may be grumpy and rude sometimes, but he showed up without hesitation when he thought I was being hurt...and then he stuck around to take care of me. Even after my bully of a dog attacked him.

My stomach flutters at the reminder of Carter swooping in to save me, and then flutters again when his hand tightens around my breast. My nipples tighten, heat of an entirely different kind suffusing my body. He said he wasn't sleeping with me yet, but he made it pretty clear that he wants to sleep with me.

I may be a virgin, but I'm almost positive he didn't mean that in the literal sense. He wants to have sex with me. Fuck me? Make love? Whatever. He wants to get me naked and do dirty things to me. Who cares what he calls it? Especially since I'm pretty sure I want to let him get me naked and do dirty things to me. After I pee and brush my teeth.

I wiggle like a worm, trying to inch out of his hold, but he mumbles in his sleep again and pulls me closer, practically lying on top of me so I can't get away. His face goes to my neck, his free hand drifting down my hip to squeeze my ass.

He grinds his dick against me and groans. "Goddamn, you smell good, princess."

"You're awake."

"So are you. Do you feel better?"

"Yes. I feel fine now. Where's Peter?"

"I let him outside about an hour ago. Last I checked, he was passed out on the couch."

"You let him out? What time is it? He's probably hungry."

"It's almost five, and he's fine, sweetness. I already fed him."

Butterflies start dancing in my stomach. Even though Peter tried to murder him, he still took care of both of us while I slept the day away. Why does that turn me on so much?

"You're in my bed," I whisper.

His lips touch the side of my neck, curving into a smile. "So are you."

"Are you naked?"

"Yes."

"You're naked in my bed."

Jeez. Master of the obvious much, or what? Get it together, girl.

"Unfortunately, I can't say the same about you being naked," he mumbles against my skin, making me shiver in a good way. "We can change that."

Yes, please.

"I need to pee. And brush my teeth. And definitely shower. You said I smell good, but I'm sweaty and I bet my hair is probably a mess. Um...I should probably do other stuff too, but I can't remember what right now. Why are you laughing?"

"Luna?"

"Carter."

"Go pee before I roll you over and fuck you into tomorrow, princess." His lips brush my shoulder and then he reluctantly releases me, flopping onto his back.

I quickly roll to my feet, and then stumble when I catch sight of him. He's definitely naked. "Christ on a cracker," I whisper, staring at his cock. It's standing straight up and it's way bigger than I thought it was...and I didn't think it was small to begin with. "There's no way I can have sex with you. You'll break me in half with that thing."

His cocky smirk makes my lady bits quiver again. He wraps one hand around his cock and strokes it, his eyes heated. "Oh, I'll fit, princess."

"I'm a virgin," I blurt out.

His hips jerk and a little spurt of come seeps from the head of his cock. "Fuck," he growls, groaning loudly. "You better go do what you need to do, Luna."

"Why?" I cross my arms and scowl at him. Now that he knows I'm a virgin, he wants me to leave the room?

"Because if you don't, I'm going to have you naked and screaming for daddy to make you come in about two seconds," he says, still working his hand up and down his cock. And good grief...did he just say he wants me to call him daddy?

My stomach dips, heat flowing through me at the thought. Why is that so hot? Who cares? Suddenly, I don't have to pee so badly. I'd rather stay right here and get to the screaming part.

I've seen porn before, but watching him jerk off is different. My whole body tingles. I'm pretty sure my panties might have exploded too. I stare at him, fascinated and turned on as he masturbates, staring shamelessly at my body the whole time.

"Luna, go," he growls.

"Fine." I throw my arms up in surrender and stomp toward the bathroom. "Hot, grumpy, bossy jerk," I mumble under my breath. I'm pretty sure he hears me though, because he chuckles before the bathroom door closes.

I stand there for just a minute, my heart racing. I kind of want to dance around and celebrate the fact that Carter is naked in my bed and obviously wants to have sex with me, but that probably isn't very ladylike, so I don't do that.

I quickly take care of business and brush my teeth while the shower heats. As I feared, my hair is a disaster. I tame the unruly curls as fast as I can and then hop in the shower to wash up.

"Carter!" I yell when he slides in behind me, crowding me up against the wall by seaming his body to mine.

"You were taking too long," he says, tipping my chin up with a finger. His green eyes are darker than normal, his cheeks flushed. "I missed you."

My entire body melts.

"Did you brush your teeth?"

I nod.

"Good, then I can finally do this," he grunts and then his mouth crashes down on mine. His tongue flicks against the seam of my lips, demanding entry. As soon as I let him in, he groans, spearing a hand through my hair to tilt my head back further. He doesn't seem satisfied by that because I'm still at a weird angle. Why is he so much taller than me?

"Carter!" I yelp, wrapping my arms around his neck when he picks me up like I don't weigh anything at all. "Stop picking me up. I'm too big."

"The hell you are," he grunts and then bites my bottom lip, dragging it through his teeth. "Do you have any idea how fucking hot you are, princess? Your sexy little curves drive me crazy." He rocks his hips into me as if to prove that he finds me attractive. "I could carry you around all day and not get tired."

That's because he's the Hulk, but I don't tell him that. Instead I dig my hands into his hair and bite his lip, moaning. I'm so turned on I think I might actually combust. He wraps my hair around his fist, tilts my head back, and then claims my mouth with a possessive, hungry kiss. His brandy and sugared spice taste is like a drug, instantly addicting.

I get lost in the kiss and the way he clutches me to him, his hard body plastered to mine. Or maybe mine is plastered to his...I'm not sure. All I know is that my legs are around his waist, his lips are on mine, and these greedy little growls rumble in his chest. I'm drenched in desire and wriggling all over his hard cock.

And then he slips his free hand between us to capture one nipple between his thumb and forefinger. His cock presses against my clit as he grinds me against him. He pinches my nipple and I fly apart, shouting his name as a powerful orgasm blasts through me out of nowhere. It's way bigger than anything I've ever given myself. My entire body lights up and then liquefies.

"Fuck, princess," he groans against my lips before pulling back to rest his forehead against mine. "I need to feel that on my tongue and then my cock."

I don't think that was a question, but I answer him anyway. "Yes. Oh my gosh, Carter." I dig my nails into his shoulders, trembling as aftershocks continue to shoot through me. It feels so good. No wonder people are always talking about sex. If it always feels like this, it's awesome.

He turns like he's going to carry me out of the shower.

"I didn't wash up," I mumble.

"Sweetness, I'm just going to get you dirty."

"Yeah, but..."

"But what?"

"We can't have sex if I'm already dirty," I whisper, my face flushing. "I mean, we probably can have sex if I'm dirty, but I had a migraine earlier and I feel gross. I don't want to remember feeling gross my first time."

He cocks his head to the side and stares at me for a full minute before he smiles, his dimple flashing. "You're right. Let's clean you up, and then I'll get you dirty."

I beam at him, relieved.

He presses a sweet kiss to my temple and then slides me down his body. Once I'm on my feet, he grabs my body wash and dumps it onto a purple loofah before scrubbing me down, his tongue caught between his lips like he's really concentrating on his task. By the time he's done, I'm trembling with desire.

"Feel better now that you're clean?" he asks.

I nod emphatically.

He shakes his head and smiles at me before turning the water off. "Hang on to me," he murmurs, and then picks me up again. He sets me down long enough to dry us both off and then sweeps me up into his arms again.

I wiggle for him to put me down, but he smacks me on the ass and then nips at my shoulder. "Settle down before I fuck you against the wall. I want you in the bed the first time so I don't hurt you."

My body melts again. Maybe I'm crazy, but I think I love him. He may be grumpy and a little rude, but he's so damn sweet. I'm crazy, right? Oh, who cares? He's naked, I just had the best orgasm ever, and I'm pretty sure he's about to take my virginity.

"'Kay," I mumble, nuzzling my face into his throat as he carries me into the bedroom. And then I nip at his skin like he did me. He tastes good. I bite him again.

He growls, tossing me toward the bed.

I cry out in surprise when I hit the soft mattress and bounce.

He latches a big hand around my ankle and yanks me until I'm flat on my back with him standing over me, his green eyes on fire and his fist wrapped around his cock. "Let me see what's mine, Luna."

I bite my lip and slowly part my legs. My face heats. No one but my gyno has ever looked at me down there. I didn't even know that was a thing guys wanted to see. But judging by the look on Carter's face, he definitely wants to see. Part of me wants to clamp my legs together and cover my breasts, but then he growls, licking his lips. I part them further, opening myself to his hungry gaze.

"Anyone ever put their mouth on you before?" he asks and then clenches his jaw. "Fuck, don't answer that. It'll just piss me off. Doesn't matter if anyone has before. You're mine now. I'm the only one who will ever eat your pussy after this."

"I've never..." I swallow hard, refusing to feel embarrassed about this or think too deeply about what he means about him being the only one ever. He didn't mean forever-ever. It's too soon for that. Right? "I've never done anything. Well, I mean, I've made myself come before. But no one else has ever done that to me or anything. Except you. You made me come. But you were there for that so..."

His expression softens as I ramble, warmth filling his eyes. "Good. I'll be the only one who ever eats you then." He seems satisfied by that, like he really does mean forever-ever. His eyes heat, his tongue swiping along his bottom lip. And then he lunges, burying his face between my legs.

I cry out, shocked and turned on beyond belief as he spreads my lower lips apart and then groans so loud he sounds like a snarling bear. A really hot, really muscular, and not-at-all-furry bear.

"So soft and pink," he mumbles, lifting me toward his mouth. He eats me like I'm the best thing he's ever tasted. It's loud and messy, wet sounds and his growls and curses ringing around the room. His fingers dig into my ass, spreading my cheeks apart as he thrusts his tongue inside me.

Oh my God. I never knew I could feel this way. It's like Christmas and my birthday and Halloween are all happening at once inside me. Bliss flows through my entire body until I'm sobbing and clawing at the sheets, trying to get closer to his mouth. He sucks my clit into his mouth, thrusting two fingers into my opening and then curling them up.

An orgasm blasts through me, making me scream.

Carter growls again as another flood of moisture flows between my legs. He licks it all up, not stopping until I practically crawl up the bed, trying to get away from his mouth. I'm so sensitive I think I might pass out if he keeps it up. And I don't want to pass out yet. He hasn't even de-virginized me yet.

He lets me go with a displeased rumble, only to rear up over me on his knees. His expression is absolutely feral, his eyes blazing. His face is soaked with my juices. That probably shouldn't be as hot as it is, but it is. Sexy. He uses the back of his hand to wipe his face and then falls forward, catching himself on his hands before his big body crushes mine.

His lips descend on mine, his kiss slow and sweet. I can taste myself on him. The combination of his flavor and mine is kind of hot. I'm not sure if I'm supposed to think that or not, but I do. I moan into his mouth, wrapping my arms around his neck to get closer to him.

He hitches my right leg up over his hip, the broad head of his cock sliding through my folds. "Going to take you now, sweetness," he murmurs against my lips when his cock nudges at my entrance. "It'll hurt for a minute, but then it'll be good for you, okay?"

I bob my head up and down on the bed, grasping his shoulders and clinging. Nervousness ripples through me, followed by a mix of anticipation, excitement, and genuine worry that he isn't going to fit. But I want this. I think I need this more than my next breath.

I want this man to be my first and my last. My forever-ever. Why does that sound less crazy every time I consider it?

"Condom!" I blurt out at the last second, proud of myself for re-membering. Because, yeesh! It's hard to think when his hard body is over mine and he's kissing me.

"No condom," he growls.

"I'm not on birth control."

"Good." He bites my bottom lip before soothing the sting with his tongue. "I'm taking you bare, sweetness. When I'm in you, I'll always be bare."

"But..."

"I'm going to breed you," he whispers, nipping my ear and then moving back to my lips to kiss me again. "I want you round with my baby so everyone knows you're mine."

My entire body clenches at the thought of this man getting me pregnant. "Yes," I moan, wrapping my legs around his waist so he knows I'm more than happy with that plan even if he doesn't mean forever-ever. I bet his babies would be so beautiful.

He presses forward, slowly stretching me. I dig my nails into his shoulders, whimpering. He's so big. It hurts. Tears sting my eyes as something stretches and then tears, sending a sharp pain through me. I whimper again, digging my nails into him so deeply I'm sure it's probably hurting him too.

"God, you're tight, princess," he says on a hiss, an intense look of pleasure and pain on his face. He continues to push forward until he's sheathed inside me, his hips resting against mine. He stays still then, pressing gentle kisses to my cheeks and eyes. "It's okay. You're doing so good for daddy, sweetness. I promise it'll be better soon."

I jerk my head in a nod, hoping he's right.

"Kiss me," he whispers against my lips.

I obey his command, kissing him until I'm breathless and the pain dulls to pleasure. Even then, he doesn't stop kissing me. Not until I retract my nails from his shoulders and start wiggling around for him to move. I feel so full of him. It's like he's everywhere—inside me, on top of me, wriggling his way into my heart. His scent swirls around me, relaxing every muscle in my body.

"Oh," I whisper in surprised pleasure when he slides out and then rocks his hips to push back into me. Pleasure spirals out like ripples in the ocean. It feels so good. Like when his mouth was on me, only better.

"You like that, princess?"

"Yes," I moan.

He tips his head down, smirking at me. "Good. That's real good, sweetness," he growls. He rocks his hips into me again, pulling my leg higher up his hip. The change in angle makes me writhe beneath him. He grunts and rocks faster, pounding into me. "This is the only cock you'll ever know, Luna. When your pussy gets needy, it's my cock you'll beg to have fill it. When you're coming, it'll be my cock you drench. You're my princess and I'm your daddy now."

"Carter!" I scream, bucking beneath him as he fucks me hard, his hips slamming into mine. Hearing him call himself my daddy only makes me want more. The bed shakes like it might collapse, but I'm pretty sure it's sturdy enough to hold up. I guess we'll find out.

He grinds against my clit, sending pleasure striking through me like lightning. It sizzles against my clit and then burrows deep into my womb, reverberating through me from head to toe. I forget about the bed. Forget about everything but him.

"Fuck, your little cunt is gripping me like it was made for me, princess." He leans down, pulling one of my nipples into his mouth. His teeth clamp down on it, sending another jolt of pleasure through me. "Knew you'd feel perfect wrapped around my cock. Going to keep you on it as often as possible. When you need to come, you'll climb up on my lap and sit on this dick, Luna. It's yours now, so take it like a good girl and let daddy breed you."

"Yes, daddy!" I cry out, sobbing my agreement. So long as he keeps fucking me like this, I'll give him anything he wants.

"Cream for me so I can fill your tight little cunt up with my seed, princess."

I didn't know it was possible to orgasm on command, but I do, screaming his name. Lights flash behind my eyes before the entire world goes black. My body convulses beneath him, held down only by the way his hips pin me in place. Blood rushes through me in a loud roar, my heart pounding fiercely.

I peel my eyes open in time to see Carter throw his head back, roaring my name. His hips jerk, his body going taut as he comes, spilling into me in warm spurts. He fills me up until it spills out, sliding down the crevice of my ass. I writhe beneath him, aftershocks ripping through me each time he moans my name, calling me his princess.

Eventually, he falls forward, burying his face in my throat. He keeps his weight off me with his forearms. His body is sweaty. He trembles, pressing a sweet kiss to my throat. "Goddamn, Luna," he breathes, panting in my ear. "I'm ruined, sweetness. Completely ruined."

"Me too," I mumble, my eyes sliding closed.

"Good," he whispers.

I'm in so much trouble with him.

Chapter Five

Carter

"Are you pouting?" Luna asks, narrowing her eyes on me from across the kitchen.

"No," I lie, crossing my arms over my chest to glare at her. I'm totally pouting. I woke up hungry, but she wouldn't let me eat her again. I don't know if it's possible to survive on pussy and orgasms, but I'm more than willing to give it a shot. In the name of science, of course.

But I probably should feed her first. It's close to midnight, so I know she has to be starving. And she's already little. I can't convince her to marry me if she wastes away because I didn't take good enough care of her.

The reminder that she's mine to take care of now has me prowling toward her across the kitchen. Once I reach her, I wrap my arms around her waist and pick her up, sitting her on the island. "What do you want to eat, sweetness?"

"You're going to cook for me?"

"Said you were mine, didn't I?" I mumble, tucking her hair behind her ears so I can see her face. She's so damn beautiful. Like my own fairy princess. Maybe I should send Psycho Layla a gift basket to thank her for driving me out of my last apartment and into the path of Luna. "If you want me to cook for you, I'll cook for you. Whatever you want, you get now, princess."

She turns those big eyes up at me, her lips parted like she doesn't know what to say. The happiness in her gaze makes my dick hard all over again. I kiss the shit out of her and then reluctantly pull back.

"What do you want to eat?"

"I can cook," she says, slightly breathless.

"So can I. What do you want?"

"Anything." She bites her lip like she's having second thoughts about that. "Maybe eggs and toast?"

"I can do eggs and toast." I pull on the handle of her fridge, but instead of opening, the handle comes off in my hand.

"What the fuck?" I scowl at the handle.

Luna giggles. "My apartment is kind of a hot mess."

"Fucking Danvers," I growl. "Trying to wheedle his way in here with you."

"He is not." Luna throws a kitchen towel at me.

I catch it, turning to look at her. "He is," I tell her, dead serious. "He's a pervy old bastard, sweetness. If anything else breaks, you call me to fix it, not him."

"He's harmless," she says, her voice soft.

"Don't care," I mumble, stomping toward her. I tip her head up until she tilts it back, meeting my gaze. "Promise me you won't let him in here without me, Luna."

Her gaze flits across my face for a moment, searching for something. "I promise," she whispers.

I press a grateful kiss to her forehead and then release her. It takes me a minute to find her tools underneath her sink to fix the fridge door, and then I have to tighten the screws on one of her drawers, and the knobs on her faucet.

By the time I'm finished, I'm steaming mad. I bet that fucker comes in here when she isn't home and messes with shit so she'll have to call him for help. Not anymore. I'll be making a stop by his office first thing tomorrow to tell him to keep his old ass out of my girl's apartment or I'll rip his throat out.

I wash my hands and then get started on her eggs and toast. She directs me around the kitchen from her seat on the counter, her expression soft.

"So you like eggs, toast, tiny dogs, gangster rap, and fantasy creatures," I murmur after getting the eggs going. "What else?"

"I don't like tiny dogs," she says with a soft laugh. "I like big dogs, but Trevor gave me Peter for Christmas as a joke."

"Trevor?" Who the fuck is Trevor and why is he giving my girl a dog?

"My brother. Well, one of them. I have three." She scrunches up her nose, scowling. "They're all older than me and try to boss me around."

"But you don't let them do that, do you, sweetness?"

"Nope." She beams at me again. "I moved here to remind them that I'm the boss of me."

"Yeah? Your family doesn't live here?"

"No. They all live in Santa Maria. My parents own a few vineyards. The boys run a winery and restaurant. Well, Trevor and Eli do. Nathan does some kind of super-secret tech research. What about your fami-ly?"

"My parents are currently in Europe," I say with a smile. "They spend half the year trekking around the globe, and the other half in their beach house in Santa Monica."

"Oh, I want to travel!" Luna kicks her feet back and forth. "I think seeing the world would be so much fun. Especially New Zealand. It's so pretty there. I could probably come up with all sorts of ideas in New Zealand."

I make a mental note to take her to New Zealand and then flip her eggs and start the toast. "You're the artist responsible for all those drawings in your room, princess?"

"Yeah," she says, suddenly shy. "I do illustrations and graphic design for books."

"Is that what you went to school for?" I grab Peter's food and fill his bowl when he comes barreling into the room like a tiny streak of lightning and starts jumping around at my feet, trying to get my attention.

"No. I went for business management."

I cock a brow, surprised by that. She doesn't seem the type to be happy in a cubicle or office. She's too free-spirited for that, too bright. "You're incredibly talented, Luna. Don't plan your life around a job that stifles your spirit. You'll be miserable."

"I know, but I want to be able to help out with the vineyards. Eventually, my parents will pass them on to us. When the time comes, I want to be ready to do my part."

I add selfless to the list of things I know about her.

The toast pops up.

Peter jumps and growls for a second before he goes right back to eating, making Luna laugh.

"Do you like your job?" she asks as I grab plates and dish up the food, slathering butter on the toast for her.

"It's a pain in the ass most days, but yeah, I like what I do." I hand her a plate and then pour us both a glass of orange juice before leaning back against the counter across from her with my plate in hand. "I like solving problems."

"I bet you're good at it."

"I don't suck."

She smiles like she's proud of me, which makes me feel ten-feet tall and bulletproof. "Do you have any siblings?"

"I have a sister. Her name is Cadence. She's a teacher in San Francisco. Eat, Luna."

She makes a big production out of cutting a piece of egg off and popping it into her mouth. And then she moans around her fork, her eyes rolling back in her head. "Either these eggs are amazing, or I'm starving," she says with a little laugh when she notices me staring at her. Her cheeks turn pink.

I groan at the sight, tipping my head back. "Fuck. You gotta stop getting embarrassed around me."

"Why? I get embarrassed a lot. It's because my mouth works sometimes before my mind does. Like when I said something about your um..." She waves a hand at my crotch. "Which is way bigger than it looked the other day, by the way. And it didn't look little. Obviously you don't take steroids, and I'm sorry for suggesting you do."

Fuck, I love her.

"Luna."

"Carter."

I chuckle at the way she pitches her voice low like she's trying to imitate me. She sounds like an asthmatic chain smoker instead. Not sure how anything about that is cute or a turn on, but my dick twitches anyway.

"Why do I have to stop getting embarrassed?" she asks again.

"Because every time you blush, I think about the fact that your cunt is the same shade of pink as your cheeks. It makes me fucking crazy."

She chokes on her toast.

"Shit." I drop my plate to the counter and hurry toward her, grabbing her glass of juice as she coughs so hard her eyes water.

She takes a sip, coughs again, and then takes a deep breath.

"You okay?" I ask, worried about her.

"Did anyone ever tell you that you say really inappropriate things?"

"Oh? *I* say really inappropriate things?" I arch a brow at her, smirking. "You really want to go there with me, princess?"

"I don't say inappropriate things!"

"You mentioned climbing me like a tree, insulted my parents, and talked about my cock the first time I met you," I remind her.

"You thought my dog was my boyfriend."

She squeals with laughter when I lunge for her, tickling her until she screams for mercy.

"You win!" she cries, pushing me away from her. "You win."

"Damn straight I do," I growl, and then kiss her hard on the mouth before moving back to my spot to finish eating.

"I've never had a boyfriend before," she says a few minutes later.

"Good." I rinse my plate and drop it in the dishwasher before taking hers from her to do the same. The thought of her with some other guy pisses me off. I don't want her to even think about other men. Ever.

"Hey, Carter?"

"Yes, Luna?" I glance her way.

"Um..." She shifts around, glancing at me and then away. "Um...what are we doing?"

"Right now? We're cleaning the kitchen so I can take you back to bed to fuck you again." I close the dishwasher and pace toward her, not stopping until she has to spread her legs to allow me to stand between them. "But that's not what you were asking me, is it?"

She shakes her head, hiding her eyes from me.

"Luna?"

"Carter."

A smile tips my lips up. The way she says my name is so fucking cute. I hook a finger under her chin, tipping it up until she looks at me again. "I'm getting to know you so I can convince you to marry me and have my babies, sweetness. That's what we're doing."

"Oh." A huge smile overtakes her face. "Okay."

"You good with that plan?"

"Yes, daddy," she whispers, wrapping her arms around my neck.

"Danvers," I say, stepping into the business office on my way in to work the next evening. He's passed out at the desk, his head back and his mouth wide open. I reach out and kick the leg of his chair, making him jump.

He sits upright, blinking at me through bleary eyes. "Carter? Is something wrong?"

"Not so long as you understand me," I mutter. "You sober enough to have a conversation about how you're going to stay the hell away from Luna Goodson's apartment so I don't have to break your jaw and then take you to jail for harassment?"

He scrubs a hand through his hair, his mouth opening and closing like a fish out of water.

"Don't even try to tell me you didn't intentionally undo half the screws in her kitchen."

He eyes me for a minute and then chuckles. "Well, shit, son. What'd you expect? She's a sweet little thing, and damn fine to look at." He shrugs, all bashful like. "Plus her cookies are fucking amazing."

"She made you cookies?" Jealousy and anger rip through me at the thought, followed immediately by guilt. She's too goddamn innocent to even realize this old fucker wants in her pants. I can't be mad about that. I love that she sees the world through rose-colored glasses. It's a good thing she's mine now though. She clearly needs someone looking out for her.

"I wouldn't say she made them for me. Just that she shared them with me." He shrugs again like it's no big deal and then tips his head to the side, studying me. "She yours now?"

"Yeah, she's mine now."

"Does she know she's yours?"

I grit my teeth at the suspicion in his voice and then nod. I've made it more than clear to her where this thing between us is heading just as soon as she lets me take it there. I'm fucking crazy about her. Hell, I have been since day one.

No one has ever made me feel like she does...like I want to tattoo my name on her and lock her away so no one else gets any of her time but me. I also want to give her every single thing she's ever wanted, and spend at least three-fourths of each day with her coming on me. My fingers, my tongue, my cock...doesn't matter which.

Danvers narrows his eyes on me. "Then you might want to let the lady who keeps coming around here looking for you know that," he says. "Don't think Luna would appreciate finding out she's yours while some other lady still thinks you're hers."

"What lady?"

"Tall, leggy blonde with a tight ass. Looks like she could suck the chrome off a bumper. Leah? Leia?"

"Layla?"

He snaps his fingers. "That's the one."

"She's been here looking for me?"

Danvers nods.

"Jesus fucking Christ," I growl, my stomach turning. The woman is a stone-cold psycho. I'll be filing for a restraining order as soon as possible. I don't want her anywhere near Luna. Who knows what she might do? "If she comes back around, kick her ass out of here. She's not to go anywhere near my apartment or Luna's."

His bleary eyes clear a little, wariness creeping in. "She going to be a problem?"

"Not for long," I mutter. "Do me a favor if she comes back?"

He nods.

"Call me as soon as you see her."

"Will do," he agrees.

I head out, wishing like hell I could spend the night in Luna's bed instead of at work. Having her all to myself for the last day and a half wasn't nearly long enough. The next twelve hours are going to be complete torture.

Chapter Six

Luna

"Peter, it's too early to go out," I groan, pushing him away when he pounces on my chest and starts licking my face. I didn't sleep very well. Probably because I spent half the night trying to finish up a project I didn't get done because I've been spending all my free time with Carter lately.

It's been a week since he took my virginity, and if he isn't at work, he's with me. I don't think he'd leave my apartment at all if he didn't have a job. Well, that's not true. He did take me to the movies and to dinner when he was off on Friday. And then we took Peter on a hike on Saturday.

Carter ended up carrying him the entire way because the little bully decided he didn't want to walk anywhere. I swear, he spoils my dog as much as he spoils me.

I told my mom about him. They even talked on the phone. She likes him a lot. She hasn't said a word about him to my dad or brothers. They'd all come racing down here to give him the third degree. And I don't want them scaring him off like they've scared off every other guy that's ever had an interest in me. Not that I had any interest in any of them, but still. If it was up to them, I'd die a virgin spinster with six cats and a wicked little dog.

Peter bounces on my chest again, barking at me.

"Fine," I mutter, pushing him off and sitting up. "I'll take you out. But only because I need to get up anyway and not because you're a bully." I think he's gotten worse since I met Carter. I can't even be mad though because he looks so damn handsome toting around my tiny dog. He even brought Peter home a bunch of new toys yesterday.

Peter jumps from the bed and starts running in circles in the floor.

I roll out of the bed and pull on one of Carter's t-shirts and a pair of my sleep shorts, though the shorts aren't really necessary. His shirt is big enough to cover me. But last time I tried to take Peter out in nothing but Carter's shirt and a pair of panties, he spanked me and then fucked me until I couldn't move.

My stomach dips at the reminder, heat flowing through me.

I grab my phone off the bedside table to see that it's a little after eight. A big smile overtakes my face when I see I have a text from him.

Carter aka Grumpy: Something came up and I'll be late, sweetness. You better be naked and wet for me when I get home. I've been hard all night thinking about you.

I hug my phone to my chest like a lunatic and then head to the bathroom to take care of business. Peter runs around in circles the entire time, barking at me like he's telling me to hurry up. He's so impatient.

I slip a pair of flip-flops on and then follow him downstairs with the pooper scooper and waste bags in hand. The railing on the stairs doesn't wobble anymore. I guess Carter fixed it. Oddly enough, everything else in my apartment seems to be working fine now too. I hate to cast aspersions on Mr. Danvers' character, but I think Carter might have been right about him.

Which makes me a little sad. Mr. Danvers is probably lonely. I don't think he has many friends or any family. He's a little odd and always smells like alcohol and stale cigarettes. It's probably off-putting to most people. But he seems harmless to me. I mean, he always stared at me a little weird, but he never crossed any lines.

Peter hikes his leg to pee on the bushes and then bounds across the grass, chasing after a butterfly. I watch him for a minute and then call my mom.

"Morning, little bird."

"Morning, mama." I smile. She's been calling me that since I was little. She says it's because I'm always flitting around like a hummingbird.

"What are you doing up so early?"

"Your granddog is a spoiled little terrorist."

She laughs quietly. "I told Trevor not to get you a small dog, but he didn't listen to me. He said you'd fall in love with him."

"I do love him," I admit, watching as the butterfly alights on a tree. Peter tries to jump up the tree after it, barking and growling. "But he's still a terrorist."

"Where's your man at?"

"He's still at work. Did you know more crimes are committed in the summer than in the winter? I always thought people would be crazy during the holidays, but they're not. Well, I mean they are, but they're less crazy during the holidays than summer. Maybe they feel bad about doing crime in winter because it's the birthday of Jesus. I bet they don't want to go to hell."

"Schools are out during the summer, little bird," Mom says, laughing. "Having bored kids at home all day will drive any parent to insanity."

"I didn't drive you crazy."

"No," she agrees, still laughing. "You didn't. You drove your brothers crazy and then they drove me crazy complaining about you and all the reasons I should lock you up in the house all summer."

"It's not my fault they all think they're the boss of me," I mutter. If I tried to wear a bathing suit, they would have a fit. What else was I supposed to wear at the pool though? A nun's habit? Older brothers are so annoying!

"It's because they love you, little bird. You know those boys would do anything for you. Speaking of which...are you going to tell them about that man of yours anytime soon?"

"Um...no?" Is she insane? As soon as they find out about him, there will be no stopping them. What if he meets them and they scare him off? I don't think he scares easily, but he's never met my brothers before either. They're all big bullies. I don't want them to scare off Carter.

"Why not?"

"Because they'll scare him off."

"I don't think that'll happen," she says, a smile in her voice.

She's probably right, but why risk it?

"Why don't you bring him home for the 4th? I'll help run interference and make sure they don't act up. They may be grown, but I can still strike the fear of God into them if need be."

She's definitely right about that. The boys hate to make her mad.

"I'm not sure if he can take off work, but I'll talk to him about it," I agree, knowing it's inevitable. I mean, I could be carrying Carter's baby for all I know. We've had sex a ton of times without a condom because he keeps telling me he wants to see me round with his baby. I can't resist him when he says things like that. My ovaries swoon and then he's giving me orgasms and I forget that condoms even exist. But meeting my family should probably come before springing a pregnancy on them...right?

Crap.

Mr. Danvers steps out of the office on the far side of the parking lot. I lift a hand to wave at him. He waves back but doesn't come to talk to me like he normally does when I see him out and about. He heads in the other direction. I think Carter said something to him because he's been avoiding me all week.

Why aren't I angry at Carter for trying to be the boss of me? When he does it, I don't think it's annoying. Well, I mean, it is a little annoying, but it's also kind of sweet. It's not sweet when the boys do it. Only when Carter does.

"Hey, mama?" I ask. "How did you know you were in love with dad?"

"Oh, little bird," she says with a soft laugh. "If you're asking me that question, I think you already know how you feel about Carter."

"I'm in love with him," I whisper, peeking around to make sure no one is close enough to overhear. Which is silly. It's not like any of my neighbors would run and tell Carter anything. This isn't kindergarten. But aside from a pretty blonde sitting in a Mustang in the parking lot, there's no one else out here. She's been staring in my direction for a while, but I don't know her, so she probably isn't looking at me.

"I know you do," my mom whispers back.

Peter gives up trying to get the butterfly out of the tree and finally does his business. Once he runs back to my side, I cross the grass to clean up after him and drop it in the waste-bin set up at the edge of the courtyard.

"He said he wants me to have his babies," I admit, and then flush bright red.

"Oh, dear."

"What?"

"I think you definitely better bring him home soon, little bird."

"I'll talk to him," I promise again.

"Call me soon and let me know, okay?"

"Okay. Love you."

"I love you too, sweetheart. And I'm so happy for you. I know your dad and your brothers will be too if you give them a chance."

She's right, darn it.

"I need to get you a key so you don't have to knock," I say, pulling open the front door with a big smile when Carter knocks half an hour later. Except it's not Carter standing outside. It's the blonde who was in the Mustang earlier.

"Um, hi. Can I help you?"

She flicks her icy blue eyes up and down my body, her lip curling. "I'm here to see Carter."

"Oh. He isn't here right now."

"When will he be here then?"

"I don't know. He's at work. I can tell him you stopped by though," I offer, crossing my arms over my chest. I don't like the way she keeps looking at me like I'm a bug she wants to squash. She's really pretty, but her eyes are puffy like she's been crying. I can't just shut the door in her face even though I kind of want to do exactly that. "Are you okay? I'm sorry. I don't know your name."

"It's Layla."

"I'm Luna."

"I know who you are," she says.

"You do?"

"Did he tell you that I'm carrying his baby?"

My heart stops beating.

"I didn't think so," she says, her lip curling up again. "Typical. He kicks me to the curb for you, but doesn't even tell you that he's got a kid on the way. When he gets home, tell him I thought about his offer, but I'm not getting rid of the baby."

I put my hand on my throat, trying to make myself breathe. I feel like air is frozen in my lungs, refusing to move through my bloodstream.

"A word of advice?" Her cold gaze flicks up and down my body again. "Don't get too attached. He talks a big game, but once he gets what he wants from you, he'll drop you like you're nothing and come back to me. He always does." With that, she turns and storms off, her heels clicking on the cement.

I slam the door closed, sliding weakly down the front of it. Someone else is pregnant with Carter's baby. He told her to get rid of it.

Is this what heartbreak is supposed to feel like? Does it always hurt this badly?

My hands go to my stomach, cupping it protectively. I don't even know if I'm pregnant, but the thought of him even asking me to get rid of our baby rips my heart apart. Why would he do that to Layla? How could he?

A sob breaks from my lips.

Oh my god. I'm in love with him...and some other woman is carrying his baby.

She said he always goes back to her after he gets what he wants. What if that's what he's planning to do with me? Leave me to go back to her? Why wouldn't he? She's practically a freaking supermodel, and she's carrying his baby.

My heart rebels at the thought, refusing to believe he would do that to me or that he's cruel enough to demand Layla get rid of his baby. He's so good to me. He's kind and considerate, and goes out of his way to make sure I'm taken care of. He hasn't said he loves me, but he always says he's going to convince me to marry him.

She's pregnant.

It doesn't matter if I love him or not. It doesn't even matter if he loves me or not.

He should be with Layla and their baby.

I have to let him go.

I climb to my feet, blinded by tears. My entire body hurts as I stumble toward my room, desperate to get out of the apartment before he gets back. There's no way I can face him right now. Not when my heart is shattering in my chest.

Chapter Seven

Carter

"Did you finish that report?" Lieutenant Davidson asks, poking his bald head into my office.

"Finishing it right now," I mutter, not even looking up from the computer screen. It's almost ten in the morning, and I'm exhausted. Some jackass got hopped up on meth last night and decided to rob two convenience stores and carjack a little old lady. But granny was packing too.

She shot him in the chest, killing him instantly.

I spent half the night processing the scene and questioning her and all the witnesses. The poor old woman is devastated. It took hours to convince her that she wasn't going to prison before I was finally able to get her statement.

"You need anything else from the patrol guys who responded?"

"Nah, I've got everything. Give me five to spellcheck and I'll have this ready for you."

Davidson nods. "Head out once you get it finished, Grayson. I told the desk you'll be coming in late tonight. You know Chief is on his bullshit about all the overtime."

"When isn't he on his bullshit?" I mutter, making Davidson chortle. My cellphone rings.

"I'll let you get that," Davidson says and then ducks out of my office.

I snatch the phone up, hoping it's my girl calling. Leaving her at home to come to work every night is the worst kind of torture. Knowing she's snuggled up in bed without me, her tiny tank top riding up and her shorts barely covering that juicy pussy makes me crazy. If she doesn't fall in love with me soon, I'm going to lose my mind.

"What the fuck?" I mutter, frowning when I see it's Danvers calling and not Luna.

"Hey, Carter. Sorry to bother you, but well, you told me to call you if I see the blonde again," he says as soon as I answer.

"Yeah?"

"Well, I just saw her leaving Luna's apartment," Danvers says, sounding confused. "I thought I was mistaken, but I'd know that tight ass anywhere. I can identify anyone based on the size and shape of their ass. It's like a superpower."

"She was at Luna's apartment?" I growl, worry shooting through me.

"Yes. Well, maybe? I didn't see her at the apartment, but she was coming down the stairs. She left in a blue Mustang. I wouldn't have even mentioned it, but you told me to call you so..."

"Fuck. I'm on my way." I disconnect and then hit save on my report before grabbing my keys and jumping to my feet. I dial Luna's number, but it goes straight to voicemail. I stop walking long enough to fire off a text, telling her to keep her door locked and to call me back immediately.

I hurry out of my office, not even taking the time to close the door. Layla was at Luna's and now my girl isn't answering the phone. Dread sits like a weight in my stomach, worry for Luna overriding everything.

"Davidson!" I shout when I see him walking toward his office down the hall.

He turns toward me.

"The psycho I told you about last week was just at my girl's apartment," I tell him, jogging down the hallway. Last week wasn't the first time I've mentioned Layla to him. He knows she's the reason I moved out of my last place. He personally served her with the protection order two days ago. We still have to attend a hearing later this month, but until then, she isn't supposed to come anywhere near me or Luna. I didn't want to scare Luna so I didn't tell her, but I should have. Fuck. If that bitch hurt her because of me, I'll never forgive myself.

"Is your girl okay?"

"I can't reach her. She's got her phone turned off, which she never does."

"Fuck," Davidson says, his expression grim. "Go. I'll get a squad car started over there and be right behind you."

"Tell all units to keep an eye out for a blonde driving a blue Mustang," I mutter, not sticking around for anything else. I take off toward the parking lot, running full out. My heart is in my throat the entire time. I try to dial Luna again, but it goes straight to voicemail.

If Layla did something to hurt her....

Fuck, I can't even think about it without a wave of pain blasting through me.

I hop in my Explorer and crank it, hitting the control box to activate the lights and sirens. My tires squeal as I pull out of the parking lot, racing toward the apartment complex. I try to dial Luna again and then again, but it goes straight to voicemail each time.

"Fuck, princess, pick up the phone," I whisper. The drive is only five minutes, but it's the longest goddamn five minutes of my life. By the time I roar into the parking lot, my blood pressure is so high I'm sweating.

I pull up crossways in three spaces and slam the car into park before jumping out. I don't even bother to shut the door before I take off toward the stairs, running as fast as I can.

"Luna!" I yell, pounding on her door. "Luna, open the door."

Peter barks from inside, so I know she's still in there. She wouldn't leave him alone.

"Luna!" I slam my shoulder against the door, trying to force it open.

"I've got the keys!" Danvers shouts from below, jogging across the grass toward me. His beer belly bounces as he runs, and he has to hold his pants up with one hand. He's red in the face and panting before he reaches the bottom of the stairs. He tosses the keys at me as a patrol car flies into the parking lot.

I snatch them out of midair and spin back to the door, shoving the key into the lock. Peter goes crazy, barking and jumping around, as soon as I have it open. He growls at me and latches onto my boot. I reach down and pick him up to soothe him, but he's not having any of it today.

"Knock it off!" I growl when he clamps down on the side of my hand. His teeth are so small he doesn't even break skin, but it still pinches like a motherfucker. I tap him lightly on the nose with my forefinger to get his attention.

He yelps like I just tried to kill him and then goes limp in my arms. Swear to God, he's the most overdramatic little shit I've ever met. I sit him on the couch and then race toward Luna's room.

"Luna! Where are you, princess?" I shove the bedroom door open and a pencil comes flying at my head from the far side of the room. I duck just in time. It sails past my head and hits the wall. I freeze when I catch sight of Luna, relief filling me. She's safe. That crazy bitch didn't hurt her.

"Don't touch me!" she cries, backing away when I stomp toward her. Tears fall down her face in a flood, breaking my heart. Her eyes are red and swollen. And then I notice the suitcase on the bed and her clothes all over the floor.

"Luna, princess. What's going on? Talk to me."

"Don't call me that."

"Why not?" I whisper, moving carefully toward her. She backs up another step, which breaks my heart in half. Not once has she ever backed away from me. The fact that she's doing it know kills me. I'm going to lose my mind when I find out what that bitch did to upset her.

"Were you even going to tell me?" Luna asks, her voice cracking.

"Tell you what?"

Before she can answer, Peter starts going nuts again, alerting me to the fact that someone else is in the apartment.

"Don't you even think about moving," I growl at Luna before stomping back to the living room to wrangle her demon dog. He's got his teeth clamped around the leg of Davidson's pants, growling like the little savage he is.

Davidson just stands there looking at him in shock.

"Peter, enough!" I snap at the dog.

He growls once more and then releases Davidson before padding toward me.

"What the fuck is that thing?" Davidson asks.

"A demon spawned in hell," I answer, making him laugh. I reach down and pick Peter up in one hand. "He's her fucking guard dog. He thinks he's a Rottweiler."

Peter grins at me, clearly pleased with himself.

"Your girl okay?"

"She's safe."

"What happened?"

"I'm still trying to figure that out."

Davidson nods. "Lewis stopped Layla about three minutes ago. I'll tell him to hold her while you sort it out."

"Appreciate that," I mutter, heading back down the hall toward Luna. I drop Peter off in her office and close the door so he doesn't attack anyone else. The last thing Luna needs to deal with right now is her dog being put in dog jail for biting someone other than me.

Once he's secured, I stalk toward the bedroom, determined to find out what the hell Layla said to my girl and why my girl is packing like she's leaving me. Because there's no way in hell I'm letting that happen. Not today or any other day.

Chapter Eight

Luna

I dump an arm full of panties into my suitcase and then hurry back to the dresser to get bras and socks. Carter stomps into the room, slamming the door closed behind him.

He's breathing hard, his chest rising and falling rapidly as he glares at me. Even angry, he's so damn handsome. There are dark shadows beneath his eyes like he's tired. Tears fall faster down my face as he looks between me and my suitcase. A mix of pain and anger fills his green eyes.

"You aren't fucking leaving me," he growls, taking two steps toward the bed. He grabs my suitcase and dumps everything out of it before stalking past me with it in his hands.

I try to wrestle it away from him, dropping all of my bras and socks in the process.

"You're not the boss of me!" I yell, glaring daggers at him over the suitcase when he refuses to let it go. "I can go anywhere I want to go."

"Fine. Then I'll go with you," he says.

"You can't!"

"Why the hell not?"

"Because…because someone else is pregnant with your baby!" Anger turns to sadness at the reminder and my voice cracks as a sob breaks from my lips. I release the suitcase, trying to spin around so he can't see me crying. It's bad enough that a freaking supermodel is having his baby. I don't need him to see me with my nose red and my face streaked with tears.

He doesn't let me get away with it though. He tosses the suitcase aside and grabs me around the waist, throwing me over his shoulder. I kick my feet for him to put me down, but he just smacks me on the ass and stomps toward the bed.

I don't know what else to do, so I do what Peter would do. I sink my teeth into his shoulder and bite him.

"Did you just bite me?" he growls, tossing me onto the bed.

"You're trying to kidnap me. Help! Stranger danger! Stranger danger!" I yell, trying to roll off the far side of the bed.

He's a lot faster than I am though. He flips me onto my back and then straddles me, keeping me pinned beneath him. And now is not the time to get turned on, but he looks so hot looming over me like some angry, sexy bear.

"I moved you three feet, so it's not kidnapping. And I'm not a stranger, Luna," he says, and I think his lips twitch with amusement before he remembers he's angry at me. "I'm your man, your daddy."

"No, you aren't."

He growls at me again, his eyes narrowing on me. "Say that shit again and I'll blister your ass, princess. Don't fuck with me right now."

"Then get off and let me go!"

Where's my bully of a dog when I need him? He wants to eat everyone's face off until I need him to eat someone's face off, and then he disappears. The traitor.

"That will never happen," Carter says, leaning forward until our faces are inches apart. A muscle in his temple throbs as he glares at me. "I will never let you go, Luna. You are mine. I fucking love you. If you try to leave me, I will find you and drag your sexy ass right back here because I know you love me too."

I freeze, barely even daring to breathe as hope crashes through me. "You love me?" I whisper.

"Like fucking crazy, princess." He presses his forehead to mine, exhaling a shaky breath. "I've never felt this way before. All I think about is you. If you're happy. If you're eating enough. If you're warm enough or had enough sleep. If I'm giving you enough orgasms or if I should try for one more. Always, I'm thinking about you, worrying about you. When I'm sleeping, I even dream about you."

My entire body melts, and then my heart breaks again. Tears fill my eyes, spilling over. "It doesn't matter," I whisper, choking back a sob. "We can't be together. I won't be the reason an innocent baby grows up without a father. And it was really cruel of you to tell her to get rid of it, Carter. How could you do that?"

He rears back like I slapped him. "You think I got her pregnant and then told her to have an abortion? What the fuck, Luna?"

"She said..."

"Don't give a fuck what she said," he growls, putting his hand over my mouth. Anger flashes in his eyes, turning them a stormy green color. "I never fucking touched that woman, Luna. She was the property manager at the last place I lived. She kept breaking into my apartment while I was at work. I found her naked in my bed one morning when I got off. I kicked her ass out and moved the very next day."

My heart fills with hope.

He grabs my hand and presses it against his groin. Even though he's angry and I'm crying, he's hard. "This is for you, princess," he says, his voice rough. "I hadn't touched another woman in months before you. Couldn't even get hard for another woman. You're the only one he wants. From the second I saw you, you've been the only thing that gets my cock hard. The only one I think about."

Now probably—definitely—isn't the time, but I squeeze his cock anyway. I can't help it. It's right there, and so hard, and my hand just closes around it, trying to work him through his pants. It's a sickness. One I don't want to ever get over. I want him. Forever-ever.

He groans, pulling my hand away from him. "If she's pregnant, the kid isn't mine, Luna. And I would never tell a woman to get rid of my child. Even if that woman wasn't you, I would fight through hell to keep my baby safe. You know me, sweetness. You know I wouldn't do some fucked up shit like that."

He's right. I *do* know him and he wouldn't do that. He might be grumpy and rude and bossy, but he isn't cruel. Just look at how he is with Peter. The dog is certifiably insane, but Carter still dotes on him. He doesn't even get mad when Peter tries to attack him. He just picks him up and pets him until he calms down again. Because that's who Carter is. He's the sweetest, kindest man I've ever met. There's not a cruel bone in his entire giant body.

"Carter," I cry, feeling like the world's worst person ever as the truth settles over me. Layla isn't pregnant with his baby. How could I doubt him? "I'm sorry. I'm so, so sorry."

"Shh, princess," he whispers, shifting around until he can pick me up and put me in his lap. He wraps his arms around me, holding me close while I sob into his shoulder, apologizing over and over for doubting him.

And then I remember that he said he loves me. My sobs slow and then halt. I pull back to look up at him. "You love me? Are you sure? I mean, I'm loud and I get nervous and say really inappropriate things and I love dragons and fairies and hobbits and I listen to rap music and insult your parents. Maybe you should think about this for a while."

He eyes me for a moment and then shakes his head like he doesn't know what to do with me. "I don't love you despite all of those things, Luna Goodson. I love you because of them, sweetness." He brushes his thumbs under my eyes, drying my tears with a soft smile on his face. "I love you. Even when you're a mess. *Especially* when you're a mess."

"I'm always a mess," I mumble.

"Yeah," he says with a little laugh, "you are. But you're my mess."

"Carter?"

"Luna."

"You don't have to keep trying to convince me to marry you. I love you too." I bite my lip, looking up at him. "That's why I was leaving. Because I love you and didn't want you to have to choose between me and a baby."

"The only babies I'll ever have are the ones you give me, princess," he whispers, brushing kisses all across my face. "Your tight little cunt is the only one I'll be coming in until the day I die. It's the only one I've ever been in bare."

"I love you, Carter."

"I love you too, sweetness."

Chapter Nine

Carter

"Carter," Luna moans, writhing beneath me as I tease her clit with the tip of my tongue. She's sprawled out across her bed, her thick thighs spread wide and her full breasts on display. Her face is flushed my favorite color pink and her long hair flows across the pillows. She looks like my very own dirty fairy, ready to be claimed.

I suck her clit into my mouth, flicking my tongue across the hard nub in teasing strikes that have her sobbing *daddy* so loud I'm sure the neighbors hear her. I don't give a fuck. If she wants to scream the walls down around us, I'm more than happy to let her do it. At least that way, every other motherfucker in this complex knows she's mine.

My cock throbs when I release her clit and press my tongue against her tight little asshole.

She screams my name in shocked surprise, and then clutches at my hair as if to keep me right there. I flick my tongue against her little hole without breaching that entrance. I'll get in there later, claim that hole too. But that's not what I'm after right now.

I thrust two fingers into her cunt, rubbing them across her g-spot. She orgasms almost instantly, her sweet juices flooding my mouth. She tastes so damn good. Like moonlight and candy. I bury my face in her pussy again, drinking it all up.

She convulses beneath me, practically ripping my hair out. I don't even care though. Fuck, she's so goddamn hot when she's coming. I don't even know how it's possible for her to get any sexier than she already is, but she does. When she comes, she transcends simple sexiness, hitting some entirely new level of perfection.

I keep at her until she falls limp beneath me, and then I kiss my way up her body, paying careful attention to her fat nipples.

"Mmm," she moans when I take her mouth in a deep kiss.

"You taste yourself on me, princess?"

Her cheeks flush.

"Don't be shy. I fucking love how you taste. So damn sweet."

I kiss her again and then move back, flipping her to her hands and knees. She droops forward, putting her upper body to the bed and lifting her hips higher.

"Carter!" she gasps when I smack her ass.

"That's for trying to leave me today," I growl, my cock pulsing as her creamy white skin turns pink. I smack her other cheek. "That's for biting me." She writhes beneath me, thrusting her ass up higher for more. "That's for saying I'm not your daddy." I bite my lip at the sight before me and smack her ass again. "And that's for doubting me."

I think about giving her another smack for yelling stranger danger, but I don't because that shit cracked me up. Davidson heard it from the living room. He was practically in tears laughing when we walked out of the bedroom to deal with the Layla situation.

I don't think she'll be bothering us again. I wanted her behind bars for daring to come close to Luna, but my girl is far too forgiving. She convinced me to have Layla admitted to a psychiatric facility for observation and evaluation instead of hauling her off to jail. She'll be there for a while.

From what I understand, she isn't pregnant, but she genuinely believes she is. She's also insistent that her imaginary baby is mine. I hope they're able to help her.

If they don't and she comes back...well, I don't think we're going to have any problems getting the judge to sign off on a permanent order of protection after the events of the day. The woman is certifiably insane. She had pictures of me all over her home. Even had a few little things that had gone missing from my old apartment without my notice. If she comes near us, she'll go to jail for stalking and violating the protection order.

Luna is safe and she's all mine. We're going to Santa Maria in a few weeks for the 4th. I plan on asking her to marry me while we're there. I figure I should probably ask her father before I put a ring on her finger. Her family is important to her, so they're important to me.

As for my family, they can't wait to meet my girl. I had to forbid my sister from driving down to meet her days ago. I promised she could come to visit on my next weekend off. My parents are flying home in early July and are already making plans to stay for a while.

"Daddy," Luna whines. "Fuck me."

She doesn't have to ask me twice.

I grasp her hips in my hands and thrust into her, not stopping until I'm balls deep. The broad head of my cock nudges against her cervix, which makes her cry out in a combination of pleasure and pain. Her tight pussy grips me like a glove, pulling a loud groan from my lips. Swear to Christ, she gets tighter every time I'm in her. Her greedy little pussy clamps down around me like it's trying to keep me nine deep inside it.

I pound into her hard and fast, transfixed by the way her plump ass jiggles and bounces with each deep thrust. Spreading her cheeks apart with one hand, I groan at the sight of her little pink hole. Until her, I was never an ass man, but goddamn. Hers is perfection. I play with that little hole with one hand, sliding my other around her hip to strum against her clit.

Her head flies back, a startled groan ripping through the room when I push the tip of my finger into her.

"You feel that, sweetness?" I growl, fucking her like a madman. "Feel how you clench around me like your little asshole is begging me to fill it?"

"Oh god, Carter."

"That's because this little hole belongs to me too, Luna." I push my finger inside her, my balls drawing up as a bolt of possessive satisfaction courses through my veins when I've breached that hole, claiming it too. "You're my little fuck princess. Even your body knows I'm your daddy now, sweetness. You belong to me."

"Yes!" she cries out, writhing all over my cock. "Yes. I'm yours, daddy."

Fuck. Hearing her call me daddy does something to me, makes me absolutely feral with the need to possess this woman. I can't even explain it. I've never wanted anyone else to call me that, but with her,

I need it. I love being the one who keeps her safe and meets every need she has.

Possessive desire and adoration roar through me in tandem, annihilating everything but her. I thrust into her again and again, my balls striking her ass with heavy slaps.

She cries out over and over, her tight cunt clamping like a vise around my cock. "Please, daddy, please," she pleads, tearing at the sheets with her hands as she writhes and moans, so close to going over the edge. I'm right there with her. Fucking desperate for it.

"Come for me, princess," I growl, playing with her asshole and her clit until my stomach clenches, an orgasm barreling toward me. "Your little pussy is hungry for my seed. Come so I can fill it up."

"Yes!" she screams, her sweet voice cracking as she breaks for me.

Her cunt grips onto my cock, her walls fluttering like a hummingbird as she goes wild beneath me, coming harder than she ever has before. Watching her orgasm sends me catapulting over the edge into my own. My hips slam into hers, a roar leaving my lips as I come hard, my balls draining into her tight pussy in powerful spurts. It overflows, sliding down the insides of her thighs and onto the bed below.

I keep pumping into her, not stopping until I'm completely drained and she's limp beneath me. She's drenched in sweat, her sexy body trembling with aftershocks. I collapse beside her, rolling her so I don't have to leave the heat of her body.

She cuddles into me with a sweet little sigh.

"Luna," I whisper, pressing my lips to her shoulder. "My princess."

"Carter," she whispers back, her voice drowsy. "My daddy."

My heart rolls, love for her filling me to overflowing. I bury my face in her hair, breathing deeply. "I love you, sweetness."

"I love you too. Forever-ever."

"Forever-ever," I agree, smiling.

Epilogue

Luna

<u>Seven Years Later</u>

"Mommy?"

"Arwen." I glance in the rearview mirror to find my oldest daughter looking at me from her car seat, her little nose scrunched up like she's deep in thought about something. There's a smear of paint across her cheek. Her dark hair is wild, her bright green eyes wide. Unlike their older twin brothers—Bastian and Jareth—who look exactly like Carter, Arwen and her little sister, Hermione, are a perfect mix of me and their daddy.

"What's a gat?" Arwen asks.

"A gat? Where did you hear that?"

"In a song."

"What song?"

"The one daddy listens to with the guy with the funny name. Small Bigs."

"Biggie Smalls?"

"That's what I said," she huffs, rolling her eyes. "The song said he was packing gats." The furrow between her brows deepens. "Did he mean cats?"

"Um...yeah, maybe," I lie, narrowing my eyes. I'm going to strangle Carter when we get home. Arwen is five. Way too young to be listening to Biggie! She already asks a thousand questions a day about everything under the sun. Now she's going to start asking about bitches and hoes too. I can't explain bitches and hoes to a five-year-old! I don't even understand bitches and hoes myself.

"Oh." She gets quiet for a minute. "Why was he packing cats?"

"Maybe he was moving and wanted to take them with him?"

"Oh, okay." She smiles, her expression clearing like she finds my explanation entirely reasonable.

I exhale a deep breath when she doesn't ask anything else, and turn by the vineyard to head home. Before the twins were born, Carter moved us out of the city. We're back in Santa Maria now, on a tract of land right outside of my family's vineyards. Moving back home was an easy decision to make once we found out I was pregnant. I wanted to be closer to my family, and Carter wanted me as far away from Layla as possible after she was released from the psychiatric hospital.

My brothers are oddly accepting of Carter. Probably because the first time he met them, he told them he loved me and there wasn't a damn thing they could do to run him off. They tried anyway, but he refused to budge, making it clear he wasn't going anywhere. They backed off after that and welcomed him to the family with open arms.

I think they like knowing I'm married to a bossy brute of a man. It certainly doesn't hurt that they all found their own women shortly after I met Carter. Now they spend their time bossing around their wives instead of me.

Carter works for the police department here, which is going to make it harder to get away with hiding his body. Is homicide justified if your husband lets your five-year-old listen to gangster rap? I'm not sure, but I'll Google it later. I'll borrow someone else's phone to do it. Just in case I need to cover my tracks.

The front door opens and he steps out with the twins and Peter hot on his heels. My heart dips toward my stomach and my nipples tighten at the sight of my man. He looks so handsome in his tight t-shirt and jeans. His hair is shot through with silver now, but he's just as hot as ever. And even bigger.

He spends a lot of time working in the vineyards with my brothers, learning the ropes. My parents announced their impending retirement a few months ago. Carter says he wants to be ready to do his part so I can focus on my art. He still spoils me like I truly am his little fairy princess, giving me everything I could ever possibly want and then more. He's shameless when it comes to me.

His lips tip up into a smile as he and the boys jog down the steps to us. The boys go straight for Arwen, helping her out of her seat. They're good boys. They're only a year older than she is, but they're as overprotective as their daddy and uncles. Luckily, Arwen is more than capable of sticking up for herself. She has them both wrapped around her little finger.

She's going to drive them insane when she's older.

"You are in so much trouble," I tell Carter when he opens my door and pulls me out.

"Yeah?" He smirks, wrapping me up in his arms. "I hope it's the dirty kind, princess."

"Your daughter asked me about packing gats on the way home."

He buries his face in my hair, his body vibrating with silent laugher.

"It's not funny, Carter!" I growl, swatting him on the shoulder. "I don't know how to explain gangster rap to her. She's a little girl! When she gets in trouble at school for talking about bitches and hoes, you're going to the parent-teacher conference to explain yourself. Oh my God. What if she starts telling Hermione about bitches and hoes?"

"Luna, princess." Carter pulls back to look at me. His green eyes dance with humor. "Hermione isn't even two yet. I doubt she'd even understand if Arwen tried to talk to her about bitches and hoes."

"Stop saying bitches and hoes," I hiss, jerking my head toward the kids. The boys have Arwen out of her seat. Bastian has her backpack slung over his shoulder. Jareth is trying to tie her shoe for her. Peter dances around at their feet. Surprisingly, he's really good with the kids. I was worried at first, but he took right to them, deciding he was their little guard dog as much as mine. If anyone so much as makes them cry, he goes ballistic.

"They aren't even listening to us," Carter points out.

He's right. They aren't. The boys are focused on Arwen, listening as she rambles on about her day and all the books she borrowed from the library for them to read. They've both got their dark heads bent toward her, listening intently. The sight makes me smile. They're so good with her. Even when she gets excited and doesn't make any sense, they just nod their heads and agree with whatever she says.

Carter hooks a finger under my chin, turning my face until I'm looking at him again. "It was one song, sweetness. I promise it didn't stunt her mental or emotional growth. She'll be okay." He rubs my belly. "Now stop getting all worked up before you make yourself sick. My baby girl is cooking in there."

My irritation evaporates as he rubs my pregnant belly, staring at me like I'm the center of the universe. I'm pretty sure that the kids and I are the center of the universe as far as he's concerned. He's so good to all of us.

"You're such a good daddy to us," I whisper, leaning up on my tiptoes to kiss him.

He growls against my lips before pulling me closer. His cock nudges insistently against my belly. My panties instantly get damp, desire coursing through me. Seven years later and we still can't keep our hands off each other. When the kids are down for the night, he's on me, fucking me until I pass out. It's better every time. As soon as I call him daddy, he loses control. I love it and so does he. Which is precisely why we already have four kids with another on the way.

"Fuck, princess," he growls, nipping at my lips. "You taste so damn sweet."

"Daddy," I whine, reaching between us to stroke his cock through his jeans. With my back to the car and the car between us and the kids, they can't see what I'm doing to him. "I need you in me."

He sweeps me up in his arms without hesitation. "Boys, why don't you take Arwen inside and read her a story before dinner?"

"'Kay, dad," Jareth says.

They all take off running toward the house with Peter chasing along behind them.

Carter follows them, kicking the door closed once we're over the threshold. He takes a second to set the alarm and lock the door before he peeks into the living room to make sure the boys are doing as instructed. Once he sees Bastian pulling books out of Arwen's backpack, he heads down the hall with me still in his arms.

"Panties off, princess," he growls, sitting me down on the counter in the guest bathroom and then locking the door. He reaches for his pants to pop the button and tug the zipper down. His hard cock springs free, the head a deep red color.

My mouth waters at the sight. I want him in my mouth.

"Later," he grunts when I tell him that. He lifts me up long enough to rip my panties down my legs and then he's thrusting into me.

"Daddy," I whimper and then have to bite down on his shoulder to stifle my cries.

"Goddamn, princess. You're so fucking tight." He fucks me hard and fast, reaching between us to play with my clit. Within moments, I'm on the verge of an orgasm.

"Daddy, please," I beg, writhing on the countertop.

"Not yet, sweetness. Wait for me."

I bite my lip, raking my nails down his back in an attempt to hold it off. It's no use though. As soon as he bites my nipple through my dress, I start coming. My body clamps down on his, a wave of pleasure rolling through me.

"Fuck!" His hips jerk sporadically as my orgasm sends him over the edge too. He kisses me hard, stifling my cries as his hot seed splashes inside me. I grind against him, determined to get every drop. I love the way it feels when I'm a mess of our juices. It's so damn hot knowing I'm covered in him. Even if no one else knows, I do.

"Daddy," I whisper against his lips. "I love you."

He kisses me once and then again, lingering against my lips as we both come down, breathing hard. "I love you more every day, princess. I don't know how that's possible, but I do."

He presses his lips to my forehead and then pulls back, slipping out of me with a groan. He's still hard, but he grabs a washcloth and cleans himself up before tucking his cock back into his jeans.

"No pouting. You know I'll take care of you again later," he says when he sees me pouting. Once his clothes are fixed, he snags my panties out of the floor and helps me into them.

"You didn't clean me up."

"I know." He smirks at me, his dimple popping out. "I want you covered in my come until I'm in you again, sweetness." He tugs me forward, wrapping his arms around me. We stay like that for a long moment, just enjoying our few stolen moments alone.

With four small kids, those moments don't come often.

"Daddy! Hermione is awake!" Arwen yells right on cue.

Carter releases me with another soft kiss. "Why don't you go spend a few minutes with our babies and I'll finish dinner?"

"'Kay," I agree. "I love you."

"I love you too, princess."

He snags me before I can leave the bathroom, kissing me long and deep. By the time he breaks away, my entire body is pulsing with desire and my panties are a mess of his juices and mine. He slips from the bathroom a moment later, shooting me a wink over his shoulder.

I stand there for a brief moment, smiling at how perfect my life is. I never would have imagined that Biggie Smalls would be my fairy godmother, but I think he might be. After all, he is the reason I met Carter. And I wouldn't change a single thing about it.

Her Alpha Boss Undercover

He's terrible at lying...but she's real good at making him squirm.

Nathan

Someone is out to ruin the family business and I promised my brothers I'd look into it.

Going undercover is a lot harder than I expected.

I'm a computer nerd. I have no clue what I'm doing. And I can't seem to stop watching Brooke Waters long enough to accomplish anything.

She's so beautiful, but she doesn't like me much. That's all right though. I've got all the time in the world to send those walls of hers tumbling down.

I just hope finding out who I really am doesn't send her running.

Especially since I plan to marry her.

Brooke

Our new employee is a terrible liar. He's also a bossy jerk.

He told me his name was Ben Dover...and then he invited himself to dinner with me.

I promised my boss I wouldn't tell anyone what "Ben" is really doing here, but I think Eli left out a few pertinent details. Like the fact that Ben is actually his hot older brother, Nathan. And that he's insane.

Nathan tells me that I belong to him, but no one ever wants to keep me.

I hope he's not just teasing me, because for the first time in my life, I think I actually want to be kept.

Warning

This older alpha male is crazy about his younger BBW...but she thinks he's just plain crazy in this sweet, steamy romance from Nichole Rose. If instalove, terrible liars, and over-the-top declarations make you smile, your cheeks are going to get a workout when you meet

"Ben Dover". As always, all Nichole Rose books come complete with a sticky sweet and guaranteed HEA.

Her Alpha Boss Undercover is now available!

His Future Bride

<u>Excerpt</u>

Holy shit. Cash Jamison is hot. When Kasen said he had a friend coming to talk to me about my problem with my Board of Directors, I thought he meant some stuffy old dude in an outdated suit. Cash isn't stuffy or old or wearing a suit.

He's massive, with colorful tattoos all up and down his muscular arms. His black t-shirt clings to his body, showing off the muscles beneath. His dark jeans mold to his powerful thighs. There's no hiding the bulge in them as he stares at me, his blue eyes locked on my face like he just saw a ghost. Except I don't think he'd be growling at a ghost like he is right now.

The dark rumble of sound shoots straight to my core, causing my nipples to harden and my panties to grow damp. He stares at me like he's the big bad wolf and I'm dinner. I think I'm okay with playing the role of his lamb.

"You're Cash Jamison?" I ask, certain Kase is messing with me and this is the actor he hired to play billionaire Cash Jamison. Because

billionaires don't look like this man. And Kase loves to torture me. It's pretty much his only hobby aside from pining away for Olivia, the girl he left back home.

"Yes," Cash growls. "And you're mine."

My eyes fly to his, my mouth opening into a shocked "O".

He crosses the room to me in three steps, stopping right in front of me. I tilt my head back—way, way back—to look up at him.

"Kasen didn't tell me you were a goddess," he says, his deep growl of a voice making me whimper. He shoots what I think is a baleful glare in Kase's direction. "You don't have to worry about your Board of Directors anymore. I'll take care of it for you, baby."

Whoa, Nelly.

"Excuse me?" I say, blinking at him like that's going to make him less hot and me less likely to just agree to whatever he says. Because I'm not some damsel in distress and I don't care how hot he is, I'm not just going to sit back and let him tell me what to do. No way.

"Your problem with the Board. Consider it solved," he says, still staring at me with those blue eyes that make my heart flutter. It's like they're stripping me bare and doing dirty, dirty things to me. I'm not sure exactly what kind of dirty things, but my hoohah seems to get the idea because she's wet and ready for him to slide on home.

I ignore my hoohah and cross my arms over my chest to scowl at him. "First of all, buddy," I say, resisting the urge to stomp my foot. "This is my company and I'll decide if you'll be taking care of anything for me. Second of all, I'm not your baby."

Cash grins at me, his eyes lighting up.

"And third," I turn to glare at Kasen, "I'm not bossy or dramatic."

"But you are a control freak," Kase says.

"There's nothing wrong with liking things to be organized and neat," I huff at him. "You're just jealous that I know more than you do about basically everything. Aren't you supposed to be writing a new album?"

"You do not know more than me. You just like to think you do."

"You're such a child."

"Am not."

"Go away."

"No."

"Fuck, you're pretty," Cash mutters, recalling my attention. He runs one thick, calloused finger down my cheek and then down the side of my throat. I fight the urge to shiver as electricity hums to life where he touched me, soaking my panties.

"Stop touching me." I smack his hand away.

"Why? I like touching you."

I ignore the way my stomach flutters over the fact that he likes touching me. "Because you can't just go around touching people even if you are a bajillionaire. I don't even know you. I'm pretty sure that's sexual harassment."

"His advances have to be unwanted for it to be sexual harassment," Kase supplies, most unhelpfully. He throws himself down on the sofa across from my desk, sprawling out like he lives here or something. He spends way too much time in my office. I need to find him something to do until he goes back on tour tomorrow so he'll go away and stop bugging me.

"Is that really a rule?" Cash asks, looking from me to Kasen.

Kase shrugs.

"Are my advances unwanted, little goddess?" Cash turns back to me, his expression somber.

Yes.

No.

Maybe?

I don't know. Ugh!

His Future Bride is now available!

Instalove Book Club

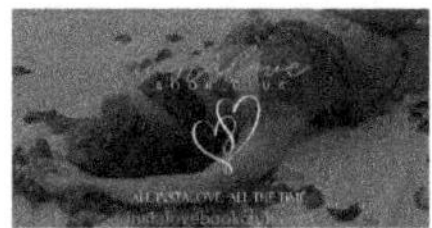

The Instalove Book Club is now in session!

Get the inside scoop from your favorite instalove authors, meet new authors to love, and snag freebies and bonus content from featured authors every month. The Instalove Book Club newsletter goes out once per week!

Join now to get your hands on bonus scenes and brand-new, exclusive content from our first six featured authors.

Join the Club:

Follow Nichole

Sign-up for the mailing list to stay up to date on all new releases and for exclusive ARC giveaways from Nichole Rose.

Want to connect with Nichole and other readers? Join Nichole Rose's Book Beauties on Facebook!

a https://www.amazon.com/Nichole-Rose/e/B0847QHXPJ

f https://www.facebook.com/AuthorNicholeRose/

https://www.instagram.com/AuthorNicholeRose

https://www.twitter.com/AuthNich
oleRose

https://www.bookbub.com/authors/
nichole-rose

https://www.tiktok.com/@authorni
cholerose

Also Available

Her Alpha Series

Her Alpha Daddy Next Door

Her Alpha Boss Undercover

Her Alpha's Secret Baby

Her Alpha Protector

Her Date with an Alpha

Her Alpha: The Complete Series

Her Bride Series

His Future Bride

His Stolen Bride

His Secret Bride

His Curvy Bride

His Captive Bride

His Blushing Bride

His Bride: The Complete Series

Claimed Series

Possessing Liberty

Teaching Rowan

Claiming Caroline

Kissing Kennedy

Claimed: The Complete Series

Love on the Clock Series

Adore You

Hold You

Keep You

Protect You

Love on the Clock: The Complete Series

The Billionaires' Club

The Billionaire's Big Bold Weakness

The Billionaire's Big Bold Wish

The Billionaire's Big Bold Woman

The Billionaire's Big Bold Wonder

Playing for Keeps

Cutie Pie

Ice Breaker

Ice Prince

Ice Giant (coming soon)

The Second Generation

A Blushing Bride for Christmas

Silver Spoon MC

The Surgeon

The Heir

The Lawyer

The Prodigy (coming soon)

The Bodyguard (coming soon)

Echoes of Forever

His Christmas Miracle

Taken by the Hitman

Wicked Saint

The Ruined Trilogy

Physical Science

Wrecked

Destination Romance

Romancing the Cowboy

Beach House Beauty

Standalone Titles

A Touch of Summer

Black Velvet

Easy Ride

His Secret Obsession

Dirty Boy

Naughty Little Elf

Devil's Deceit

Wearing their Pearls (coming soon)

<u>One Night with You</u>

Falling Hard

Model Behavior

Learning Curve

Angel Kisses

<u>writing with Loni Ree as Loni Nichole</u>
Zane's Rebel (coming soon)

About Nichole Rose

Nichole Rose is a short romance author on the west coast. Her books feature headstrong, sassy women and the alpha males who consume them. From grumpy detectives to country boys with attitude to instalove and over-the-top declarations, nothing is off-limits.

Nichole is sure to have a steamy, sweet story just right for everyone. She fully believes the world is ugly enough without trying to fit falling in love into a one-size-fits-all box. When not writing, Nichole enjoys fine wine, cute shoes, and everything supernatural. She is happily married to the love of her life and is a proud mama to the world's most ridiculous fur-babies.

You can learn more about Nichole and her books at her website .

a https://www.amazon.com/Nichole-Rose/e/
B0847QHXPJ

f https://www.facebook.com/AuthorNichole
Rose/

o https://www.instagram.com/AuthorNichol
eRose

https://www.twitter.com/AuthNicholeRose

https://www.bookbub.com/authors/nichole
-rose

https://www.tiktok.com/@authornicholero
se